GUARDIAN

"Chillingly good!"
Romantic Times

"A wildly creative, fascinating novel!"
Eloisa James for Barnes & Noble Reading Romance Blog

"You will love this series, you will love getting to know her characters and you will chill at her new world order. If you are a lover of paranormal romance, of apocalyptic stories or if you just love a great romance, give this trilogy a try."
The Reading Frenzy

"Claire Delacroix's GUARDIAN is fantastic! Delacroix artistically blends the futuristic setting with fantasy to create a beautiful and gripping story...I couldn't put this book down!"
Romance Junkies

"This exceptional follow-up to the futuristic urban fantasy FALLEN continues the saga of Lilia Desjardins' quest to locate Delilah, the daughter taken from her at birth...This exciting story kept me entranced from first page to last."
Fresh Fiction

REBEL

"Delacroix deserves congratulations for the extreme originality, both of setting and in her characters in REBEL."
The Long and the Short of it Romance Reviews

"REBEL takes the unusual mix of science, romance and religion

and make it not only work well but make it a wonderful read. REBEL definitely takes the series out with a bang!"
Paranormal Haven

"The final installment of Ms. Delacroix's trilogy is an amazing finish!... If you—like me—love romantic suspense with an urban fantasy twist, this is definitely the one you should choose."
The Reading Frenzy

"A moving conclusion to this futuristic series and a true triumph of storytelling!"
Fresh Fiction

Dear Reader;

Ideas are strange and wonderful things. Not only are they nearly impossible to anticipate, but the most unlikely ones can be the most beguiling. I had written quite a number of medieval romances when the idea behind the Prometheus Project came to me. I was skeptical of the notion of writing an urban fantasy romance with a mystery subplot, never mind one set in a gritty dystopian future, but Lilia Desjardins wouldn't take no for an answer. She was persistent and wanted her story told. Publishers also thought the idea was a risky one, given my solid publishing history in medieval romance. The editor who ultimately acquired **Fallen** *did so after I agreed to her suggestion to make the book into a trilogy. There was a lot of the Republic to explore, and I knew I could write three books set there. I also knew she was right that there should be more than one book in my publishing history in this different market niche.*

I had a wonderful time writing **Fallen**, **Guardian** *and* **Rebel**: *it was invigorating to visit new territory, so to speak, and work with different story elements than I had previously. I was fortunate to have the support of my publishing house and of my agent in trying something different. When the initial trilogy was completed, though, it troubled me that Tupperman had never had his happily-ever-after. Initially, he was a minor character, but his role grew over the series to the point that I felt I was abandoning him. The problem was that I didn't know his story.*

Several years later, ideas worked their magic again and I realized what Tupperman's story would be. I had thought that it would be a novella, but as I started to write, Tupperman's story kept getting longer. I really liked the story, so was easily convinced to spend more time in the new Republic. In the meantime, an interesting thing happened: the publishing rights for the initial trilogy returned to me. This gave me the welcome opportunity to have those three books edited again and published in new editions. I held off on publication of Tupperman's story until that was completed.

This story was initially published under the pseudonym Claire Delacroix. When I was able to license the original cover illustrations from artist Larry Rostant in 2016, I decided to make these books Deborah Cooke titles—they're a better fit with my paranormal romances written under that name than my medieval romances. Larry, of course, did illustrations for the first three books in the series for Tor, which left the question of how the fourth book would be able to look similar to the rest. I think that Frauke Spanuth did a marvelous job in creating a new cover for Tupperman's story that is consistent with Larry's designs.

*And so, welcome to Tupperman's story. It is set several years after the events in **Rebel**, when some things have changed in the Republic but others have not. The angels that Tupperman convinced to shed their wings and fight for the future of humanity have become an elite corps of soldiers called the Watchful Host. The problem is that someone is murdering the members of the Watchful Host, and worse, making it look as if Tupperman is the source of the betrayal. A disenchanted Tupperman believes that the time for his final mission has arrived, so he leaves New Gotham to meet his fate, suspecting he will never return. En route, he meets Kara, a woman who entices him and challenges him—and gives him more than enough reason to survive. It's not a spoiler to tell you that Tupperman will finally get his happily-ever-after in this final book of the Republic.*

To keep up to date on my new releases, please follow my blog or subscribe to my monthly newsletter.

Until next time, I hope you are well and have plenty of good books to read.

All my best,
Deborah

More Books by Deborah Cooke

Contemporary Romance:
The Coxwells
THIRD TIME LUCKY
DOUBLE TROUBLE
ONE MORE TIME
ALL OR NOTHING

Flatiron Five
SIMPLY IRRESISTIBLE (2016)

Paranormal Romance:
Dragonfire
KISS OF FIRE
KISS OF FURY
KISS OF FATE
WINTER KISS
WHISPER KISS
DARKFIRE KISS
FLASHFIRE
EMBER'S KISS
THE DRAGON LEGION NOVELLAS
SERPENT'S KISS
FIRESTORM FOREVER

Dragons of Incendium
WYVERN'S MATE
Nero's Dream
WYVERN'S PRINCE
Arista's Legacy (2016)
WYVERN'S WARRIOR (2016)

Urban Fantasy Romance:
The Prometheus Project:
FALLEN
GUARDIAN
REBEL
ABYSS

Paranormal Young Adult:
The Dragon Diaries
FLYING BLIND
WINGING IT
BLAZING THE TRAIL

Short Stories
BEGUILED

Claire Delacroix Books

Time Travels:
ONCE UPON A KISS
THE LAST HIGHLANDER
LOVE POTION #9
THE MOONSTONE

Medieval Romances:
ROMANCE OF THE ROSE
HONEYED LIES
UNICORN BRIDE
THE SORCERESS
ROARKE'S FOLLY
PEARL BEYOND PRICE
THE MAGICIAN'S QUEST
UNICORN VENGEANCE
MY LADY'S CHAMPION
ENCHANTED
MY LADY'S DESIRE

The Bride Quest I
THE PRINCESS
THE DAMSEL
THE HEIRESS

The Bride Quest II
THE COUNTESS
THE BEAUTY
THE TEMPTRESS

The Rogues of Ravensmuir
THE ROGUE
THE SCOUNDREL
THE WARRIOR

The Jewels of Kinfairlie
THE BEAUTY BRIDE
THE ROSE RED BRIDE
THE SNOW WHITE BRIDE
The Ballad of Rosamunde

The True Love Brides
THE RENEGADE'S HEART
THE HIGHLANDER'S CURSE
THE FROST MAIDEN'S KISS
THE WARRIOR'S PRIZE

The Champions of St. Euphemia
THE CRUSADER'S BRIDE
THE CRUSADER'S HEART
THE CRUSADER'S KISS
THE CRUSADER'S VOW (2017)
THE CRUSADER'S HANDFAST

ABYSS

DEBORAH COOKE

Abyss
by Deborah Cooke

Printing History:
Deborah A. Cooke trade paperback edition by Claire Delacroix
January 2014
Deborah A. Cooke trade paperback edition by Deborah Cooke
October 2016
ISBN# 978-1-988479-03-3

This book is also available in a digital edition.

ABYSS

PROLOGUE

From *The New Republican Record*, November 13, 2105.

Watchful Host Raid Claims Three Soldiers

New D.C.—The press office of the Watchful Host confirmed three soldiers from their elite corps were killed this morning in a raid at an undisclosed location within the Republic. The lost soldiers are Captain Rumford, Lieutenant Taylor, and Commander Stevenson. The mission is acknowledged to have been a strike against an unidentified terrorist cell. This was the fourth such incident in recent months, bringing the tally of lost commandos to eighteen. The press office dismissed any suggestion that the Watchful Host had been careless or impulsive, insisting the earthly life of every angel who has volunteered to serve for the good of humanity is precious and defended with the utmost care. All federal offices in and around New D.C. remain on Red Alert.

In a simultaneous statement, the Brotherhood of Honest Laborers declared their property and members had been attacked "maliciously and unjustly" by the Watchful Host and that they defended themselves in an exchange of hostile fire this morning. It appears likely that these separate reports refer to the same incident. The spokesperson of the Brotherhood of Honest Laborers insists that the Watchful Host has unfairly attributed recent attacks upon citizens within the Republic to their organization and undertaken covert punitive measures as a result.

The Brotherhood opposes the emancipation of those persons who had previously been known as shades. The organization has criticized the economic impact of President O'Donohue's decision to grant full citizenship to shades in January 2101. The Brotherhood claims that the introduction of so many new workers into the paid labor pool has diminished the living standard of those who were never classed as shades, or those they call "honest laborers." According to the Brotherhood, sixty percent of Honest Laborers have experienced a job loss, been overlooked for promotion and/or had their wages cut since 2101. They demand that if the shades cannot be returned to the netherzones, then they should labor only for the state and earn no paid wages.

The Oracle has condemned the policies of the Brotherhood of Honest Laborers and requested again today that they embrace the changes in the new Republic. President O'Donohue expressed his condolences for the loss and saluted the sacrifice of the fallen. Funeral ceremonies for the deceased soldiers have already been conducted privately by the Watchful Host, as is their custom.

The President announced a national period of mourning, to begin tomorrow morning at 1100. There will be a prayer from the Oracle on the hour, which will be vid-cast live, followed by five minutes of silence throughout the Republic to acknowledge the sacrifice of these warriors for righteousness. The mourning will culminate in a candlelight vigil at the shrine of the Watchful Host in New D.C. on Wednesday, November 18. The vigil will begin at 1800 and last through the following morning. On Thursday, November 19, there will be a memorial service held at the shrine at 1100. All are welcome.

Citizens should arrive early to allow time for the requisite security scans before entering the shrine of the Watchful Host. Remember that all of New D.C. remains on Red Alert and plan accordingly.

Associated Links:
Careers of Glory: <u>Captain Rumford</u>, <u>Lieutenant Taylor</u>, <u>Commander Stevenson</u>
<u>Map of New D.C. and the Shrine of the Watchful Host</u>
<u>What to Expect under Code Red Security</u>
Archive Article: <u>The Creation of the Watchful Host, an Army of Angels</u>
Archive Article: <u>The Watchful Host at Work, Defenders of Justice</u>
<u>Official Site of the Brotherhood of Honest Laborers</u>

New Gotham—November 13, 2105

Tupperman was sick at heart.

He marched through the netherzones of New Gotham, not really seeing the people around him. The underground level used by commuters was darker than usual, a result of electricity rations, but the dim light suited Tupperman's mood perfectly.

Three more dead.

Eighteen so far.

The ranks of the Watchful Host were being culled. Worse, Tupperman feared it was his fault. He had not only been the one to persuade so many of the angelic host to shed their wings and join the fight to save humanity, but he'd supplied the intelligence that had led to this particular raid on the hidden headquarters of the Brotherhood.

He'd never expected his own brethren to be killed in this realm. He'd never expected them to be targeted. This last incident had been yet another baited trap. He'd heard the crowing over those deaths on the illicit frequencies of the Republic first thing this morning and been sickened by it.

He couldn't bear his own sense of responsibility.

He walked toward his scheduled meeting, his thoughts churning as he sought another explanation, one that didn't put the blame at his own feet.

It had been four years since the angelic host had appeared in the skies over the Republic. Four years since everything should have been repaired, but it had been four years in which strife had been fueled by economic turbulence and shortages. The Brotherhood was the loudest voice of dissent, but not the only one.

It all came back to the shades.

Until recently, every child born in the Republic had been assessed under the Sub-Human Atomic Deviant Evaluation as a matter of routine. The test separated those babies damaged by radiation exposure *in utero* from the healthy population. Those babies who failed the evaluation became the property of the state, laboring in the darkness of the netherzones for the good of the Republic. For many citizens, they were out of sight and out of mind. From the acronym of the test's name—S.H.A.D.E.—had evolved the colloquial name for those humans compelled to live in the shadows.

The angelic host had healed the shades, and they had been liberated from the darkness of the netherzones. Now the former shades were citizens, but resentment in the Republic clearly ran high.

Joachim had been right.

Tupperman had been with Joachim when the blinding light of angelfire had touched the earth. Tupperman had believed his earthly quest complete but the jaded circus owner had insisted that it was not enough to set the Republic on the right path. The other man's despair for the future had convinced Tupperman to stay, although he'd never believed that Joachim would be proven so right.

Tupperman had not only remained himself: he had convinced more angels to shed their wings and take flesh in the quest to save the souls of mortal men.

And now they were being slaughtered.

Exactly where he told them to be.

The many angels who had volunteered that night had formed the Watchful Host, an elite corps reporting directly to the President and tasked with making the new Republic work. They were openly known to be fallen angels. In contrast, Tupperman's network was of angels who had shed their wings earlier and remained disguised as mortal men. He used those angels as well as a few trusted humans to find data for the Watchful Host.

But they had been betrayed.

Eighteen lost angels were already on his conscience.

How many more would there be?

Tupperman clenched his fists as he walked, frustrated that there was so little he could do. He felt volatile and cheated, angry and vengeful—all very human reactions.

"You all right, Tupperman?"

Tupperman started at the familiar voice. He spun to find Jackson, his contact at the Watchful Host, close behind him. Along with Jackson was Pierce, another of the elite corps who often attended their meetings.

Tupperman was startled. He didn't realize he'd walked all the way to his contact point. A quick glance revealed his fellows were as troubled by the morning's events as he was.

Dark-haired and dark-eyed, Pierce tended to be quiet,

thoughtful and intense. He was also keenly observant. Jackson, with his easy smile and vague air of being disreputable, was the fallen angel most at ease in the mortal realm of all those Tupperman had known. He had taken to this sphere as if it were more natural to him than the heavens he'd abandoned. He had a charm that made him easy company, but was no fool.

"I'm as well as can be expected," Tupperman said. "And you?"

"Troubled," Jackson agreed, his tone somber, and they all nodded agreement. The pair flanked Tupperman as they continued to walk, their confidence and vitality making him feel better. These were his real fellows and they would know more about whatever had gone wrong.

"What happened?" he prompted when they said nothing.

The pair exchanged a quick glance, one Tupperman guessed he wasn't supposed to notice. He felt a sudden chill, an intuitive sense that he wouldn't like what was said.

"You shouldn't blame yourself," Jackson said. "These things happen."

"Intelligence is a tricky business," Pierce said mildly.

There it was. Tupperman felt as if a shadow had passed over him. He wasn't the only one who felt he was culpable.

"Is that an accusation?" He looked between the pair, wanting his impression to be proven wrong but doubting it would be.

Pierce averted his gaze.

"We acted upon the intelligence you provided, and it was a baited trap." Jackson kept his voice light, but Tupperman heard the implication. "They knew exactly when we were coming, how many of us there would be, and our precise plan of attack. It was too accurate to be guesswork, Tupperman."

"A leak." Did they suspect Tupperman personally of betraying his kind, or someone in his network?

It was unthinkable that any of his associates could have undermined this morning's raid—he knew them all. It was also beyond belief that anyone had infiltrated his network—with Ferris and the Wraiths on his side, his security was airtight.

The leak had to be within the Watchful Host.

"It's not at our end," Jackson said with finality. "We've been over every link today, and have added layers of security since the attacks began." The other fallen angel slanted a quick glance at

Tupperman, one filled with assessment.

Tupperman was struck by Pierce's silence and took it as an indication that he had already been condemned.

"It's not like you to be fooled by anyone," Jackson added.

"I haven't been. Have you?"

Jackson smiled thinly. "Then you're trusting the wrong people. We need full access to your network and we need it immediately. We'll have to verify every one with access to your data..."

"No." Tupperman responded immediately and with conviction. If there was a leak at their end or a spy in their ranks, the last thing he wanted was to expose his own team.

He wouldn't add them to any executioner's list.

Jackson cleared his throat. "Your team needs to be fully integrated with the Watchful Host's intelligence operations, Tupperman. We've talked about this before and your resistance isn't popular."

"I have to defend them. I owe them that."

"And what do you owe us? This command is from the top, and it makes sense given recent events." Jackson spoke firmly. "You must give us access to your network."

"No." Their gazes locked and held for an electric moment, but Tupperman wouldn't be persuaded to make this choice.

Jackson's lips tightened and he looked away, as if he understood as much. "Recognize, Tupperman, that it's only a matter of time before someone begins to wonder whether you really believed the intelligence you provided."

"I wouldn't have provided it otherwise." Tupperman spoke tightly.

"There have already been suggestions that you were knowingly a part of the trap. You should know that an internal inquiry has been launched." Jackson watched him coolly. "You could be charged, and I needn't remind you that cooperation will be considered in your favor."

That he could be so quickly distrusted in the face of adversity was a shock to Tupperman, but then he was the outsider. Maybe it was easier than looking more closely within their own ranks.

Or was he being framed? Tupperman's thoughts flew. By whom? It was clear the Brotherhood of Honest Laborers didn't want to be identified, and he'd welcomed the assignment of unveiling of their members. He must be too close to the truth.

"Maybe this would be a good time for you to take a break," Jackson said serenely. Tupperman looked up as the other angel smiled but for once Jackson's smile didn't reach his eyes. "Go on vacation. I can't find any reference that you ever have."

Tupperman's thoughts flew. Jackson—and potentially others—had been through his records, and probably not just checking on his time off.

He had to save Ferris and the others.

He had to sever the only connection between the two, by breaking his own contact with both. To ensure that he couldn't be compelled to share what was in his memory alone, he had to disappear.

"Because you won't be using me for the duration of the inquiry, if not longer," Tupperman guessed quietly.

Jackson didn't correct him, which was all the answer Tupperman needed.

"A vacation is a good idea," he agreed. "You're right. I haven't taken a break in a while."

"I can arrange a leave for you. No problem." Jackson continued to smile that strange false smile.

"Thank you. I'll attend the vigil for the fallen soldiers, then go."

"Any plans?" Pierce asked, and Tupperman knew that the persons framing him wouldn't be the only ones interested in his destination.

He fought warring inclinations as they walked. On the one hand, he wanted to remain in New Gotham and hunt down the real security leak. On the other, he wanted to be as far as possible from the hub of the Republic and all its watchful eyes.

His fingers found the stone in his pocket, the one he'd found after asking to remain on that night four years before. It had been his only clue that he'd been assigned a new quest.

You will know when it is time, Turiel.

He remembered the angelic voice that had echoed in his dreams and knew the time had come to pursue this mission. The stone he carried was Trinitite. He'd discovered that shortly after finding it in his fist when he'd awakened one morning. He'd later learned that the pale green stone had been created in one location only, at the site of the Trinity nuclear test in New Mexico—when the heat of the explosion had fused the desert sand to glass. Trinitite.

He'd commence his own quest, while he still had life in his veins to do so. He'd go to New Mexico and uncover the truth he'd been chosen to reveal.

Whatever it was.

"I think I'll go to California," he lied, because the train leaving New Gotham would be the same one. "I've always wondered whether it was real."

Jackson laughed. "Sounds like a good time to find out."

The power went out suddenly and completely, plunging the netherzone into greater darkness. A shortage of electricity was one of the unwelcome legacies of the change in the Republic. Without shade labor, there was little power—or anything else. Light still came through the skylights from the street above, but the skylights were so dirty that the amount of light was minimal.

"Look at all the jobs for shades," someone cried, emboldened by the anonymity offered by the shadows. "Skylights to clean and power to generate, but that work's not good enough for them anymore."

"Not since the President set them free," said another.

"Not since the angels made the Republic a little corner of heaven."

"No, now they want *my* job," declared another man. A bitter laugh rolled through the crowd. Tupperman listened uneasily.

"They want *all* of our jobs," shouted another. "Our houses and daughters, too."

"So we can have deformed grandchildren," a woman concluded with bitterness.

There was discomfort with that last comment and a wary silence fell. Tupperman noted that Jackson and Pierce were back to back, the sight of their uniforms silencing those citizens closest to them. There was resentment in more than one face, and he took leave of his fellows, slipping into the darkness, but fully expecting to be followed.

What would he find in New Mexico? What injustice had he been dispatched to correct? Tupperman didn't know, but he trusted in the power that had sent him to this sphere. He would complete his own mission, if it was the last deed on earth he did.

I

From *The New Republican Record*, November 19, 2105.

Woman Ousted from Oracle's Residence

New D.C.—An unidentified woman was forcibly removed from the receiving hall of the official residence of the Oracle in New D.C. today. She was escorted from the premises by members of the Watchful Host, then barred from re-entering the building. She repeatedly asserted her desire for an audience with the Oracle, then called the soldiers on duty "the root of all evil." She disappeared into the crowd that perpetually surrounds the Oracle's residence before police arrived.

The Watchful Host, who are responsible for security at the Oracle's official residence, dismissed the incident. Their spokesperson said it is common for troubled individuals to seek audiences with the Oracle of the Republic, and for those individuals to become disruptive when their requests are declined. Such persons are routinely removed from official buildings of the Republic under a Code Red Security alert. The Oracle herself denied any knowledge of this woman or her presence and expressed concern for her welfare.

Links:
Amateur Vid of the Incident
Archive Item: the Ascent of the Oracle of the Republic

New D.C.—November 19, 2105

Kara was despondent. She'd run out of credits and run out of time. She would return home a failure, condemning everyone she knew and loved.

It was all because of the Watchful Host.

Although Kara had some less flattering names for them.

She marched through the train station of New D.C., not caring one bit for convention. For three weeks, she'd walked with mincing steps, kept her voice low, dressed modestly, conducted herself quietly, and followed the Sumptuary & Decency laws to the last detail. It had gotten her nowhere. She'd finally lost her temper on this, the last possible day she could try to meet the Oracle, and those angels had tossed her out.

The only mercy was that the publicly released vid of the incident was so poor. No one would identify her from it, especially since she'd left her best dress behind.

She was fed up with the Republic and its so-called defenders. All she'd asked was to talk to the Oracle. All she'd needed was a small bit of assistance. But the angels had treated her like a criminal, for daring to ask. She was more than ready to be home, with the solid earth beneath her feet and people she could rely upon on every side.

Even if their trust in her had been misplaced.

Kara winced at that truth as she strode down the train platform. She'd had two goals in coming east and had failed to achieve either. How could she have failed in both of her objectives? She hadn't been sure she'd be able to persuade the Oracle to help her people, but she'd never imagined she would be denied even an audience.

Kara sighed. It was embarrassing to recall how easy she'd believed her other goal would be. How hard could it be to seduce a man, any man, with green eyes? How hard could it be to conceive a child to fulfill the prophecy, before it was too late?

Impossible, apparently. She hadn't relied upon the revulsion that Caucasian men felt for women with brown skin. She'd thought her willingness would be enough. She'd never imagined that the prophecy's demand that the union be a willing one would become a problem.

She could have paid for an interval in the pleasure zones

otherwise.

She'd taken old herbal remedies to ensure she could conceive while she was here. She'd been ready to do anything, to say anything, to promise anything to achieve her goal. It would give her people such hope if the prophecy showed signs of fulfillment.

Hope could make all the difference in the world.

But the only thing Kara had to show for her efforts was aching ovaries. Sore feet. Wounded pride. The knowledge that she was a failure.

The Republic had won.

Again.

So-called civilization was filthy and noisy, unsettling and false. Kara couldn't wait to escape it.

She wanted to be barefoot, to be able to take a deep breath because she wasn't wearing a corset. She wanted to let her hair blow loose. She wanted to smell the wind and feel the earth's rhythm. The end of the world was coming, and she wanted to savor the few days that were left.

Instead, she'd just make it home in time.

The station in New D.C. was filled with steam and sparks of electricity as the trains were recharged at other platforms. There was a loud hum of running engines and the shouting of the men who serviced the trains. The station was dirty and crowded, people rushing in every direction and porters bellowing to each other. There were beggars and vendors mingling with passengers and children. There was baggage everywhere, it seemed.

Kara's train had arrived from New Gotham moments before and the gates had just opened for new passengers to proceed along the platform. There was some shoving as people hurried to get to the appropriate cars before the train's departure to the west. An overhead clock ticked down the seconds, timing them all. Or chiding them all. Conductors called from the ends of the cars, their voices competing with the vendors who were selling food to passengers through the windows of the train.

There was a loud hiss as the train's engines were slowed for recharging, then a shower of sparks when the engines were connected overhead to the station's power sources. The engines began to throb at a steady beat, as if the long stainless snake of the train had a heart. Kara could see the darkness beyond the end of the platform where the tracks ran shining into the night.

How far would the train have to travel before she'd be able to see the moon? It would be nearly full. At home, it would be visible everywhere, inescapable, but Kara didn't trust the Republic not to find a way to hide it.

She watched a flock of pigeons flying through the terminal, enjoying the sight of some free creature in this place. When she turned, she caught a glimpse of a man with a familiar profile in the crowd behind her.

Derek?

Again?

The crowd heaved, and he was swallowed by the throng as abruptly as he had appeared.

"Derek!" Kara retraced her steps, pushing through the people like a salmon swimming upstream. She got to the place where she thought she had spotted her husband, but there was only a porter there. He wore a coat of the same color as the man she'd glimpsed. She spun in place but couldn't see another likely candidate. The platform was emptying behind her, the rush of passengers hurrying toward the train.

"Help with your bags, ma'am?"

"No, thank you. Did you see a man here?"

The porter smiled. "I see thousands of them, ma'am."

Of course. Kara nodded and retraced her steps toward the train. She'd thought she'd spotted Derek a dozen times or more since arriving in New D.C. It made no sense. Her husband was dead, and she had no desire to see him again. She couldn't imagine he would want to see her, or that he would ever come to a place like New D.C. He had disliked cities even more than she did.

But if he was a ghost, it did make a kind of sense that he would haunt her now. Derek had always reveled in her failures, and this was a big one. Kara hefted her bag and shivered before she marched on. Even a false glimpse of him could send a bolt of terror through her.

Soon, she'd be home. A failure still, but one with honest earth beneath her feet, surrounded by those she loved and knew she could trust.

It wouldn't be too soon.

She climbed the stairs to her car, heading for her assigned seat, declining assistance on every side. Her annoyance mounted with every offer that implied she was weak and incapable of taking care of herself or a single piece of luggage. She was taller than most of the men who spoke so condescendingly to her, and she was sure she could win a fist fight with any of them.

The prospect of starting one improved her mood.

Even this last twenty-four hour train ride to New Mexico was too long to spend in the social embrace of the Republic and its rules. Kara was tempted to tear off her veils and let them see the face of a woman. She doubted it would tempt men as much as the Republic believed it would, and wanted to publicly show the rules to be wrong. She wanted to shout or do something outrageous, just to see their dismay.

She wondered what they would all think if she ran naked down the length of the train. The mischievous idea made her smile, even as the boarding passengers came to a sudden halt in the aisle.

But then she'd end up in jail and might never get home.

In fact, that kind of impulse had gotten her tossed out of the residence of the Oracle.

She just had to survive this chaos for one more day.

The line wasn't moving, so Kara peeked down the car. A woman halfway down the car was stowing her luggage while everyone behind her waited. She *did* appear to be incapable of dealing with one small piece of luggage. Several men rushed to help her, ensuring the task took four times as long as it should have. The woman's veil was so sheer that it didn't disguise her fair coloring and pretty features. Kara thought her appearance explained a great deal.

She could have found a dozen men to help her conceive a child, right in this very car.

Kara fought her frustration, tapped her toe and checked her seat assignment. She scanned the numbers on the bulkhead and located her seat just a few rows ahead. It was empty, which was a relief— she wasn't in the mood for an argument or a messed-up reservation—but the man sitting in the adjacent seat made her heart stop cold.

He was the most handsome man she'd ever seen.

Kara stared, unable to even think of doing anything else.

From this point, she could see only his head, but knew he must be tall. His features were sculpted in their perfection, his nose straight and his chin square. His lips were surprisingly sensuous. He was a man, not a boy, and one who looked commanding. Kara liked him on sight—and wanted very much to see more. His hair was cut so short that she couldn't tell whether it had been blond or silver. It caught the light around his head, looking for all the world like a halo.

She really did have angels on her mind.

She'd forgive him the association. She hated angels, particularly the Watchful Host of angels incarnate, but wouldn't condemn a gorgeous man for the illusion of a halo.

Just then, he glanced over the line and she saw that he had eyes of clearest green.

Suddenly all that had gone wrong was turned to rights. Suddenly there was a purpose driving her choices and hope for the future. Green eyes! Kara had been lost in the darkness of despair and failure, but here was a chance.

She could achieve her second goal before arriving home, against all expectation.

This man's presence—and his seat assignment—couldn't be a better sign of providence. It gave Kara a hope beyond expectation and made her heart pound. She eyed him as the line of passengers began to move again, and hoped she could make the most of this chance to fulfill the prophecy.

All she had to do was get his attention, and then seduce him. If he was resistant because of her ethnicity, she had to overcome his objections. She had to accomplish this. Kara gripped the handle of her bag more tightly. She didn't dare let this opportunity slip away. The express train would take twenty-four hours and she needed to make every moment count.

Even after her failure in New D.C., Kara could taste success.

"Angels are the root of all evil."

Tupperman glanced up when a woman claimed the empty seat beside him on the train, as startled by her pronouncement as her presence. She swept into the seat with a vigor that was remarkable for a woman dressed to the full specification of the Sumptuary &

Decency laws. She carried a large and dusty black carpetbag and dropped it before herself so that it landed with a thump.

Then she smiled at him, as if they were old friends.

The hour was late and the train had only reached New D.C. His hope that the seat beside him would remain unassigned for most of the trip had already been dashed.

Worse, she was talking about angels. She couldn't know who he was, could she? He'd dressed with care, intending to blend in with humans even more than he did usually. He'd booked the ticket in his own name, though, not wanting to give any hint that he suspected he was being set up. Someone almost certainly was following him, given the way he'd been targeted.

But this woman?

Tupperman was sufficiently intrigued to survey his fellow traveler. She was tall, maybe even as tall as he was, and dressed all in black. The skirt of her dress was cut full, then had a deep ruffle on the hem. It rustled as she took her seat and had the sheen of taffeta. He caught a glimpse of her boots and was surprised again. They were not the high-heeled laced boots that most women wore, the ones that ensured they took small and careful steps. These were boots much like his own, sturdy low-heeled boots for walking quickly or even running.

A violation of the S&D code, but one few people would notice.

Who was she?

Tupperman continued to look. Her jacket was black and fitted to show her curves to advantage. He was particularly struck by how narrow her waist was in comparison to the ripe curve of her bust and assumed she wore a tight corset.

The idea agitated him, as such ideas seldom did.

But then, he was unsettled and would be until New Gotham was far behind him.

Her gloves were long and black, made of faux leather perfectly fitted to show the elegance of her hands. He had to assume that the black meant she was in mourning, and wondered whose death she lamented. Not that of an angel, he was sure. Or did she disparage the angels to encourage some confession from him?

She wore a simple hat that seemed to exist solely to support the yards of dark netting that veiled her face. The only part of her that was uncovered was the upper part of her face, around her eyes.

They were so dark they didn't seem to have pupils. Fathomless black, with long dark lashes. A man could fall into those eyes and never return. The whimsical thought was uncharacteristic of Tupperman and he tried to dismiss it, without success.

She stared directly at him, as if willing him to look at her. Tupperman was sure he had never seen eyes so feminine and lovely. That she held his regard steadily showed a forthrightness that was unusual.

As unusual as her first words to him.

"It's what my mother used to say," she added, giving him a moment's relief. "I always thought she was kidding, but now I think she was probably right."

She gestured and Tupperman glanced up at the vid over the door to the train. The story about the ambush of the Watchful Host was playing again, part of the newscast about the memorial service.

He understood her reference, a bit late but with relief.

"I wouldn't know anything about it," he said, hoping to divert her attention.

"Everyone is talking about them," she said easily. Before Tupperman's astonished gaze, she peeled off her gloves with impatience and chucked them into the top of her bag. He blinked, unable to believe that she had revealed her hands to his view.

Fortunately for her, the people on the other side of the aisle hadn't noticed. Tupperman looked surreptitiously, well aware that the S&D laws existed so that a mortal man would never glimpse the bare skin of women.

Lest he be tempted.

Tupperman had always scoffed at the very idea, but as he looked at this woman's graceful hands, he *was* tempted. Her skin was golden brown and her fingers were elegant. Her nails were cut short and unpolished, but they gleamed with a health unusual in the Republic.

The remarkable thing was that she wore silver rings. There had to be one on every finger, some broad enough to fill a whole knuckle. They were simple bands for the most part, unadorned with gems, and they shone in the shadows.

Tupperman also noticed that she had never had a palm embedded in her left hand. The skin there was perfectly smooth.

His suspicions were roused again. Who was she? Every citizen of the Republic had routinely had a computer installed in his or her left hand, colloquially called a palm. The wafer-thin flexible communications devices had worked both ways, allowing citizens to communicate with each other and allowing the so-called Eyes of the Republic to monitor all such conversations. Palms had shorted out and been disabled when the angels had descended four years before and Tupperman, like all other citizens, now had a blank implant in his hand to replace the destroyed device and missing flesh.

This woman didn't have one. Had she been a shade? Few shades had had palms—those shades who did had been given devices with limited capabilities—and all shades had been liberated by the angels.

Tupperman risked a glance at her face, only to find her avidly watching him, as if she was waiting for him to finish his survey. He felt the back of his neck heat in self-awareness, but she smiled, apparently untroubled by his boldness. Her eyes shone with intelligence and a humor that made him self-conscious.

"Don't you have an opinion?" she asked.

"About angels?" At her nod, Tupperman felt a flicker of annoyance. "Sounds as if you have enough opinions for both of us."

She laughed then, a hearty laugh that was so genuine other passengers turned to look. "My mother used to say that, too," she admitted, her eyes sparkling.

She looked so vital and attractive Tupperman felt a surge of desire for her. He was taken aback by his own reaction.

He had never been particularly tempted by mortal women. Lust was a detail, a demand of his physical body that Tupperman usually managed with ease. He had sex at regular intervals to keep his desires in check, but one woman was as interesting in that moment as another. He had never felt the need to have a relationship. Women seemed so transparent and predictable. He could anticipate their thoughts and guess their expectations. They held no mystery for him and certainly didn't capture his attention beyond a basic attraction that could be easily satisfied.

But this woman was different. She was an enigma, at least thus far, and he doubted that his attraction to her would be easily satisfied.

If it was.

If it was even appropriate for him to be thinking of her in such terms, on such a brief acquaintance.

He wished he could think of something clever to say.

The lady showed no such limitation. Against all expectation, she offered her bare hand to him, such a breach of propriety that he thought his eyes deceived him. He stared at her hand, her skin so soft and golden, at her glinting rings and long fingers, and his desire simmered. "Since we're condemned to each other's company for the foreseeable future, I see no reason to be shy. I'm Kara."

He was perfect.

Kara felt jubilant with her good fortune. Her traveling companion would have been enticing even without his green eyes. She didn't even know his name, but she was so encouraged. She felt powerful in her femininity, a welcome change from recent experience, and was determined not to let opportunity slip away.

"Just Kara?" he asked. His tone was dispassionate but the gleam in his eyes betrayed his interest.

She spoke firmly, ensuring the conversation didn't veer into territory she didn't wish him to explore. "Just Kara."

"Do you ever see reason to be shy?"

Kara laughed, liking that he wasn't afraid to express his own opinions. "Not very often, but I doubt that surprises you."

"No, it doesn't."

Something in his voice made her look at him more closely, and she noticed the shadows in his eyes. Who was he? What had he seen in his life? "Does much surprise you?"

"No, not as a rule," he admitted. "But you already have, several times."

Kara was pleased by that. It was promising.

She might have dropped her hand then, because he hadn't yet taken it, but he removed his own glove, then clasped her hand in his. His grip was firm and his hand was warm, the press of a man's flesh against her own making Kara flush.

"I'm Tupperman," he said quickly. His breath had caught as well, a welcome sign of his awareness of her, but he abruptly withdrew his hand. Had he regretted his impulsiveness? Kara watched as he tugged on his glove once more.

She wasn't ready to let their conversation lapse, though, not after such a promising start. She lifted a dark brow. "Just Tupperman?"

"Just Tupperman." This time, he spoke with resolve.

Kara nodded approval at how similar they were. "I like it. Two simple souls, heading west, with minimal baggage and single names." She flicked a glance over him, not troubling to hide her admiration. His eyes widened slightly and a flush rose on the back of his neck. Kara let her voice drop low, to a tone of intimacy. "I think we'll get along just fine."

Tupperman held her gaze, the tension between them electric and exciting.

The train left the station with a lurch and flurry of sparks, shunting from track to track. The train car shifted to one side and then the other, and he looked out the window.

As if he had to restore his equilibrium. Kara had no intention of making that easy for either of them. She let her shoulder collide with Tupperman's at intervals, savoring the fleeting contact. They fell silent but there was a hum between them, an awareness that filled Kara with new hope.

On another night, at another time, she might have been less forward.

On this night, she had nothing to lose.

Kara put her hand on his thigh.

Tupperman inhaled sharply. He stared down at her fingers, splayed across his leg as if incredulous. Or maybe he was uncertain what the polite response might be. His throat worked, Kara noted, and she smiled at the evidence of his reaction in his trousers.

Kara laughed lightly and removed her hand. "My mother said I was too bold sometimes. I apologize if I've offended you."

"Not at all." He spoke with heat, his words falling in more of a rush than before. "Your mother seems to have said a great many things," he said and Kara laughed again. She flicked a glance at him and noted that he'd smiled in response.

"You should smile more often, Tupperman," she whispered, her voice falling low as if they exchanged confidences. Kara leaned close to him, letting her upper arm press against his. Tupperman stared at her, seeming not to breathe. If anything, his eyes had become a deeper and more vivid shade of green. "I'll tell you one more. My mother gave a prophecy that I'd bear a child with green eyes," Kara confessed. "Yet all the men I've ever known have had brown eyes."

Tupperman was visibly startled. "That can't be true."

"It is true. Everyone I know has brown eyes, just like mine. My husband even had brown eyes. And two brown-eyed people cannot make a green-eyed child."

Tupperman blinked, apparently taken aback by her bluntness. "Was your mother in the habit of giving prophecies?"

"Yes. You could say it was her business, as she was a seer."

His gaze swept over her before resolutely locking with hers once more. "And did they come true?"

"Invariably."

"Why green eyes?"

"I'm not sure." Kara sobered, because she'd thought about this repeatedly. "I think maybe such a child would be indicative of change, of new blood and maybe new ideas."

"A new beginning," he suggested, the thoughtfulness of his voice giving her pleasure.

"Maybe."

His eyes narrowed slightly as he watched her. "What does your husband think of the prophecy?"

Kara wrinkled her nose. "Nothing good!"

Tupperman was watching and waiting. He seemed to be a man not just of resolve but of patience and control. Kara liked that.

It made her want to reassure him, as well as give him something to think about.

"It wasn't what killed him, but there seemed to be a better chance of it coming true once he died." Kara shrugged. "I thought about it when I came east, of course. After all, the chances of meeting men with green eyes are much higher where there are more Caucasian men."

"Indeed."

She dared to meet his gaze again, not truly surprised to find a question lurking there. Kara's heart skipped that he had already seen the point of her confessions, and that he was already thinking about conceiving that child. She smiled at him and he averted his gaze, as if he'd been caught unexpectedly.

She could see that she had his interest, though.

"But the only men I met in New D.C. were the Watchful Host." Kara made a little growl of frustration. "With their eye shields, who knows what color their eyes are?"

He stiffened ever so slightly, and Kara wondered why. It was the second time he'd started at the mention of angels. Did he distrust them as well?

"Not to mention whether they have any interest in such intimacy," she continued easily, wondering if Tupperman could be provoked into making any confessions. "They might as well be machines for all the passion they show." She leaned closer, compelling him to meet her gaze once more, then smiled with as much invitation as she could manage. "Not like you," she added softly.

Tupperman stared at her, apparently astonished to silence.

That was better than indifference.

Kara sat back with a smile, watching how he took a steadying breath. She was no temptress, but it appeared she was unsettling her companion.

"What *about* you, Tupperman?" she asked, wanting to know more of him.

He frowned and turned to the window. "What about me?"

If Kara was supposed to be deterred, his tactic was unsuccessful. "Do you have any children?"

"No. None."

"Why not?"

He flicked an agitated glance at her. "I'm not married."

"One doesn't require the other." She smiled when he didn't look away. "Don't tell me that a fine, handsome man like you prefers chastity over passion?" She pouted a little, as if disappointed by the idea.

Tupperman blinked.

He swallowed.

His gloved fingers tightened and then relaxed, as if he was forcing himself to look composed.

But wasn't.

"I suppose I just never met the right woman," he said, his words tighter than they had been.

Oh, Kara was making great progress. She put her elbow on the armrest between them and braced her chin on it, letting her gaze rove over his features. He watched her, appearing to be fascinated. "I find myself intrigued. What kind of woman would the right woman be, Tupperman?"

She was sure for a moment that he wouldn't answer her. His silence was resolute, although his gaze searched hers.

Kara waited. She sensed that he wasn't a man who would respond well to prodding. She held his gaze, but remained silent, letting the tension grow between them. She could have sworn the air would begin to crackle or throw sparks.

Meanwhile, the train began to pick up speed as the city's lights faded behind them. Darkness pressed against the windows even when they were passing through residential neighborhoods, and the lights were dimmed in the train car, as well.

If anything, the shadows increased the intimacy of their conversation. They might have been alone, not yards away from other passengers. Tupperman took a deep breath, and she wondered if he had noticed her perfume.

Then he spoke quickly, unexpected words falling from his mouth. "She would have to be a moral person, someone who was good."

Kara was surprised. "How interesting you are, Tupperman. I am even more intrigued."

"How so?"

"You talk about a woman's morality, maybe even her character, before you mention her looks."

"Isn't it more important?"

"Not to many men. You don't have a fantasy, then, of this ideal woman's appearance?"

Tupperman shook his head. Another man might have been lying for some purpose, but Kara believed that Tupperman was emphatically honest.

"How curious. It's a woman's nature that you find alluring, not her physical traits." Kara considered this as Tupperman watched her, liking that he had surprised her. There was more to him than met the eye. Kara liked that a great deal.

She needed to test his honesty before she became too enthralled with him, before this transaction moved beyond the physical into emotional bonds. She abruptly pulled back her cuff, revealing the bare golden skin of her wrist to him.

Tupperman stared.

"So, you could find a brown woman attractive?" Kara prompted.

"You're not brown."

"What then?"

"Gold. Tawny." His voice was soft, his tone reverent. Admiring. Kara's doubts began to melt. "Tanned?" he suggested.

"No." She wouldn't take refuge in assumptions or misinterpretations. This would be clear between them. "'Native American' according to the Republic. I prefer to be called 'Indian.' I'm always this color, more or less." She eyed him, awaiting his condemnation. "Does my ancestry surprise you, Tupperman? Are you surprised to even see me on a train?"

A frown flickered between his brows, as if her questions confused her. "No. Why would I?"

Where had he been that he didn't know the truth?

Or maybe he'd never cared about anyone who wasn't Caucasian. Kara felt her eyes narrowed slightly and heard her tone harden. "They gave us numbers, just like shades, even though we were never shades. We don't usually leave our homelands anymore. That suits both us and the Republic." Her voice rose in challenge. "Could you find a woman like me attractive, if she was moral, Tupperman?"

Tupperman looked directly into Kara's eyes. "Yes," he said simply, because it was true.

His resolve convinced her that success would be inevitable.

She would have that child.

And the prophecy would come true.

Kara smiled even as her heart began to race. "Then perhaps we will get along just fine," she murmured, and put her hand on Tupperman's thigh again.

This time, he smiled and didn't look startled at all.

II

For the first time in decades, Joachim wanted a drink.

He sat at the kitchen table in his unit in New D.C., drumming his fingers on the surface with restless energy as he fought the dangerous impulse. He didn't like having visits from the authorities, and he didn't like discovering that the Watchful Host knew where he was. He'd never trusted the Republic's tendency to keep track of all its citizens, and even though he hadn't really believed that things had changed, it shook him to have his suspicions proven true.

Oh, the commando at his door had been polite and deferential, but Joachim didn't believe a word of what he'd said. Why would a member of the Watchful Host come to him to find out more about Tupperman? They were all fallen angels and should know more about each other than a mere mortal could perceive. To come to him for news was ludicrous.

Unless Pierce's mission had been something else entirely.

Joachim didn't like it. This was just another worrying incident, another facet of the new Republic that he didn't like and couldn't change. It was almost enough to make him yearn for the old days, when the Republic itself had been his opponent, when his path had been clear. He was lost without his circus and his mission, but had no idea what else he could do.

He didn't like the Watchful Host, but he didn't like that they were being killed either. He didn't like living in New D.C., but didn't know where else to go. He didn't like the rumblings he heard from the liberated shades, the simmering conviction that they were owed more—maybe even vengeance—but he was afraid to stop listening to rumor.

He felt ineffectual. Useless. Outdated. Yet as much as he despised that feeling, Joachim couldn't think of a new contribution he could make.

That he could find alcohol enticing again said much for his current state.

Joachim could hear the murmurings of the former shades who lived with him from the other room, and was glad they knew to leave him alone when he was in a mood. They adored Tupperman, because they credited him with their healing—four years before, Tupperman had sung the hymn that had summoned the angels to their small party, after all.

Joachim didn't want Tupperman to be compromised or in danger, not after the request he'd made to the angels and his own decision to stay. Tupperman was one of the good guys, one of the moral individuals who not only believed in change but tried to ensure that it happened.

Worse, Joachim didn't want to live in a world that could vilify a man like Tupperman. In fact, he'd hoped that world was gone and finding that such attitudes survived didn't gladden his heart. He pushed himself to his feet and paced the small space, reviewing his endorsement of Tupperman's character, hoping he hadn't said anything that could be misconstrued or used against his friend. He debated the merit of contacting Tupperman, but guessed that would only make things worse.

Tupperman would have seen the way the wind was blowing already and made plans.

Joachim just wished there was something he could do.

There was another rap at his door then and he jumped at the sound. He heard Marianna's sweet voice as she addressed the arrival, then her cry of delight.

Someone she knew, then.

Someone she liked.

Relief flooded through Joachim. Marianna was a good judge of character.

He realized then that she'd smiled at the commando, Pierce.

Before he could think too much about that, a familiar voice rang though the unit.

"Is he hiding on us?" Lilia demanded. "I never thought to find Joachim cowering in a corner." The former shades laughed with affection.

Joachim hurried from the kitchen to find Montgomery, Lilia and Micheline in his foyer, surrounded by the joyous cluster of his former circus performers. Montgomery waved a greeting, then reached over the group to shake Joachim's hand. Lilia worked her way through the others to hug him tightly. They both looked well, healthy and happy, and it lightened his heart to see them again.

Joachim was gruff, his joy strong enough to overwhelm him. "It's about time you turned up for a visit," he scolded. "Or did you only come to see the Oracle?" He fixed Lilia with a stern eye, knowing she would use any excuse to visit her daughter. "Maybe you're looking for a free place to stay."

"We came to see both of you," Lilia insisted. "All of you!"

Joachim saw then that Montgomery had scooped up Micheline and held the young girl on his hip. She had been one of the shades living at the New Gotham circus, until she had gone to the Frontier with Lilia. Micheline—Joachim thought she must be eight or ten— had grown taller and more confident. She had a port wine stain in the shape of a kiss on her forehead, a mark of the angels' favor, which had been bestowed on her that night four years before. She gripped Montgomery's shoulder as the others greeted her and Joachim remembered her gift of foresight.

He knew that once upon a time in New Gotham, her talent had been helpful in securing provisions for the circus. Had the angel's touch eliminated her gift?

Lilia smiled at the little girl. "Micheline said it was time for us to come to you. My mother surrendered her to us only reluctantly and only at Micheline's insistence."

"Why now?" Joachim asked.

"Angels," Micheline said in her lispy voice. "Trinity. Joachim."

"I don't understand," Joachim said. "There are no angels in the trinity."

"And you weren't part of it, either, at least not when I took catechism," Lilia teased and Joachim chuckled.

"It's all she will say," Montgomery said, more serious than

either of them and clearly mystified.

"Angels," Micheline asserted, then her voice grew more firm. "Trinity. Joachim." She gave Joachim a hard look, as if willing him to understand.

He shrugged because he didn't.

"I thought Delilah might understand," Lilia said, referring to her daughter, the Oracle.

"Got to use those family connections when we can," Joachim teased and Lilia smiled.

"How is everything?" Montgomery asked with a care that convinced Joachim that his mood might be shared.

"We're doing well enough. Come in. Have a drink." He met Montgomery's steady gaze. "I'd like to tell you about the visitor I just had."

"Who?" Lilia asked, while Montgomery's eyes narrowed.

"Captain Pierce," Marianna supplied.

Joachim nodded. "He's with the Watchful Host. He wanted to know more about Tupperman."

Montgomery and Lilia caught their breath simultaneously, then strode to the kitchen behind Joachim. Montgomery left Micheline with Marianna and the others, then closed the kitchen door behind them. Lilia, predictably, examined the unit for recording devices and wires, while Montgomery turned on the faucet so the water was running. They all three sat down and leaned over the middle of the table so they could speak in whispers.

"Tell me everything he said," Montgomery urged.

Days after their last discussion, Ferris still couldn't believe it.

It was impossible that he and Tupperman were parting ways forever, that he'd never see the other man again. But he knew Tupperman well enough to have seen his resolve in their last interview. He knew that Tupperman never spoke idly or made empty threats. He understood the older man well enough to know that Tupperman wasn't coming back.

Ever.

Ferris hadn't felt so alone in a long time. He'd met with Tupperman regularly, sharing what he'd learned and being given new assignments, and relied upon his companionship. Tupperman could have been Ferris' mentor, and he certainly had become his friend. Ferris lived as a perennial student, never quite fulfilling his apparent potential, never quite finishing his courses. His professors attributed his failure to his history as a shade.

Ferris had spent only one more day at the college before making his decision. He'd reviewed every single conversation he'd ever had with Tupperman, recalling the other man's words and sifting through them for details he'd missed. They'd recently been focused on the Brotherhood of Honest Laborers, a search that had stymied them over and over again. There had been no trail of creds to follow, no membership records that could be verified, apparently no living breathing connection—even though the Brotherhood released press releases.

Or someone did under their name.

"It's as if they only exist to cull the Host." Tupperman's once-uttered words about the Brotherhood were the ones that haunted Ferris. He came back to that sentence and the intent look on Tupperman's face as he murmured them over and over again. The older man had a talent for seeing right to the core of things.

Maybe that had been his angelic gift.

They'd dug deeper and longer in search of the truth of the Brotherhood, yet had accumulated almost nothing on the organization. What few member names they had gathered all proved to be those of citizens long dead. Ferris and Tupperman had assumed that meant they just hadn't found the right thread, but what if Tupperman was right?

What if the Brotherhood wasn't what it declared itself to be? What if it existed to eliminate all fallen angels, not just those in the Watchful Host?

If so, those records would be the perfect place to start his hunt for the spy, which meant that Ferris needed a secure place to continue his hunt. He couldn't go to Delilah, because he didn't want to bring any shadow to her life as Oracle—and besides, it was hard for him to be in the presence of Rafe, even knowing how much the pair loved each other. Ferris was always keenly aware in their presence that the fallen angel had won the Oracle's love and not himself. Although Ferris knew a number of Wraiths and might have been welcome in their refuges, he knew he had to go to Theodora and Armand. They alone would share his concerns, since Armand was also a fallen angel. There, he could work in complete confidence of their sanctuary's security and possibly have some help as well.

It took him a painful amount of time to get out of New Gotham. Ferris wanted to be sure he wasn't followed, so he headed to the pleasure zones, as if intending to lose himself in sensation. In reality, he knew it to be the most poorly mapped area of town.

After a day and night of leaving false leads and turning back on his trail, he descended into the maze of the netherzones. Those tunnels were lost to darkness and had been surrendered to rats. Ferris snuck through the sewers and finally escaped, coming to the surface only at night far from the city.

His plan solidified with every step. His mission was to find the spy. The spy would lead to the angel hunter and identifying that individual would protect Tupperman.

Perhaps save his mortal life.

Ferris owed his friend and mentor no less.

By the time Ferris reached Theodora and Armand's hidden sanctuary, his quest had been distilled to a single question. Who was the spy?

The nest was beneath an ancient barn, one that looked to be collapsing with age and disuse. He headed into it as if seeking shelter, knowing that he was being closely watched. In the darkest corner, he located the obscured door and knocked with the prescribed code.

Silence was the only response.

He turned to look behind himself, fearing he had been followed, then heard the door opening. He turned back to find a woman there, eyeing him in silence. Her hair was the brilliant hue of flame and cut so short that he could see the pale skin of her scalp. She was so fair her skin was almost white, which made the tattoos that covered much of her body look even darker than they were. She wore boots and a pseudoskin, the top of it opened and peeled back to reveal the singlet she wore beneath. The left side of her body was dark with ink, and the designs on her skin looked like machinery.

As if her flesh had been slashed open to reveal her body's inner workings.

Ferris blinked in surprise and she smiled thinly. "You must be Ferris," she said, giving the impression that wasn't a good thing.

He nodded. Ferris knew he shouldn't stare, but he'd never seen anything like her tattoos. The optical illusion they created fascinated him. His gaze fell to one on her forearm, and he realized that the slashed skin wasn't all illusion: the tattoo had been applied over and around a scar. He winced in sympathy at how painful that must have been.

When he glanced up, her eyes had narrowed slightly. She stood back with obvious reluctance, leaving just enough room for him to enter. When he did, the door was secured, then she strode past him, her manner dismissive.

"That's Tag," Theodora said, and Ferris realized she was standing in the shadowed doorway beyond. "She thinks you're leading a killer to us."

"Maybe I am," Ferris acknowledged, and he noticed that Tag glanced back at him.

"I don't trust strangers," she said tightly.

"Only strangers?" Theodora teased but Tag cast her a hostile glance.

"It's a learned response."

Ferris wondered what had happened to her, where she'd gotten those scars, what she feared, but he knew she wouldn't tell him anything.

"Fair enough," he agreed easily. "Never trusted them much myself." He pretended to be unaware of Tag and turned his attention to Theodora. "You were an assassin. If I wanted to have all the fallen angels killed, who would I call?"

Theodora pursed her lips. "How much cred would you have?"

"Let's say cost is no object," Armand suggested, appearing behind Theodora. He reached past her to shake Ferris' hand, his eyes warm with welcome. "That way, we won't overlook any possibilities."

"The Brotherhood of Honest Laborers," Tag contributed, and Ferris saw that she'd lingered to hear the conversation. She had her arms folded across her chest, which pushed her breasts to prominence. Once again Ferris tried not to stare, at either her curves or her tattoos. "They hate the angels as much they hate former shades."

"But who are they, really? Their members are all dead norms," Ferris said, showing the data chip that held all the information he and Tupperman had gathered on that organization. "I dug and dug and found only false data."

"Then we'll have to dig deeper," Tag said, appearing abruptly beside him. She flicked the chip out of his fingers, claiming it before he even realized she was there, then pivoted to march away.

Ferris made to follow her but Armand put a hand on his shoulder to stop him. "I should help," he protested.

"Tag works alone," Theodora said with a smile.

"It's better that way," Armand added. "Come and have something to eat. You must be starving. You can tell us everything while you do."

"We need to know what's happening with Tupperman," Theodora added and Ferris knew she was right.

Tupperman's heart leapt when Kara put her hand on his thigh again. His throat tightened at the sight and feel of her fingers there, her bare skin, the welcome in her eyes. He sensed her vulnerability, too, an unexpected trait in such a confident woman. It made him feel protective of her, particularly that she'd felt condemned because of her heritage. That she was outside of society made him feel a sense of common purpose with her.

Impulsively, he removed his glove and placed his hand over top of hers. He saw Kara smile as he tightened his grip on her fingers.

"We'll get along just fine," she murmured and he felt complicit in something he couldn't name.

"How far are you going?" he asked.

"New Mexico."

Tupperman was taken aback by the pleasure that news gave him. They'd be companions for an entire day, even on this express train. He found his thumb stroking the back of Kara's hand as he thought about her desire for a green-eyed child. He realized there was one facet of human nature and relationships that had never been part of his experience in this realm. He'd never fallen in love. He'd never been smitten. He'd never been consumed by desire for one woman.

Maybe this would be his last chance to do so.

Maybe Kara was the right woman.

Then he realized they had the same destination, against very long odds. He lifted his hand away from hers in sudden dismay. It was too neat, too perfect, too coincidental. He was being distracted from his objective, in a very predictable way. Like a mortal man, distracted by sexual promise.

Like a fallen angel, seduced by the pleasures of the flesh.

How could he be so foolish?

"And you? Where are you going?" Kara asked, apparently unaware of Tupperman's changed mood.

All of his suspicions flooded his thoughts anew. He had no idea who she was or what she wanted. He was letting base urges get the better of him and forgetting his own objective.

She was watching him pertly, awaiting his answer.

"Fresno," Tupperman lied, then changed the subject. "What's in New Mexico?"

"Everything," Kara said with force. "Every damn thing that matters."

He stifled a smile that she swore. She was enticing. "No angels then?"

"No, thank God." Her smile flashed again as she evidently realized what she'd said. "Maybe it is thanks to God. Either way, we're spared them at home. Well, now we are."

What was her issue with angels? If he could unearth that truth, maybe her allure would diminish. Maybe a few moments' conversation would end his fascination with her. Maybe he could discover her real intent.

Maybe her ready confessions could save him from himself.

It was an excuse to keep talking to her and he knew it, but Tupperman clung to it all the same.

The train began to rock as it gained speed and Tupperman watched Kara closely. "Now? What changed?"

She became more serious than he'd seen her so far. "The angels came once. My grandmother saw them, even though she was only a little girl." Kara lifted her hand from his thigh and raised her hands before herself. "She said they descended from the heavens, a chorus of thousands, and filled the sky with white fire."

Angelfire. Although Kara's tone carried a thread of skepticism,

Tupperman's mouth went dry. Until that night four years before, few humans had seen angels.

Were they headed to the same place because her story was linked with his quest?

She continued as he listened avidly. "It is said that no one could see anything but the brilliant light they emitted. Some people never saw again, but were struck blind by the sight. It is said that the angels possessed the secret of their radiant fire, that they shared the secret of how it could be kindled with mortal men. It is said that the explosion that turned the desert to glass was the result of their lesson."

Tupperman felt the hair stand up on the back of his neck, although he strove to remain impassive. She was talking about the Trinity test site.

His destination.

And the green stone that he had in his pocket was a souvenir of that same incident.

Who was she and how had she come to be sitting beside him on this train?

"It was our homeland, our place in the world. We were forced away from it years before, so when the angels came, we could only watch from afar." Her voice hardened. "But then we reclaimed the territory, for no one else wished to reside upon it. It was ours, our birthright and legacy, and we made it so again."

"That's where you live?"

"Yes."

Their destinations were exactly the same. Coincidence? It must be, for he had told no one of his real plans. Even his ticket was booked through to California.

Tupperman had a hard time stifling his uneasiness.

Kara turned to face him, her expression intent. "And this was why my mother said the angels were evil. Because their fire obliterated the sun and killed the life that was in the land. Their light made disease, sickened children and killed crops. Babies were born deformed among us, some so damaged that they could not survive. Because the angels gave what should never have been offered to this realm." She studied him so closely that she didn't seem to blink. "Is that not evil? And would they not be the root of it, if that were true?"

Was this true?

If the angels had been responsible for the nuclear bombs that had changed the world so drastically, then atonement must be made. How was he to right such a thing, even if it was true? How could Tupperman undo the past?

What challenge would greet him in New Mexico? Tupperman had to imagine that sacrificing his own mortal life would be the least of the price he might have to pay.

He realized then that Kara was still waiting for his answer. "I can understand the argument," he said politely.

"But you don't agree." Her gaze lingered on him for a second longer, then she gestured to the darkened vid screen with disgust. "And now they are among us again, without their wings and fire. They think they know the answers to everything and that their choices are best for all of us."

Her disdain for this idea was clear.

"You sound as if you have personal experience with their answers."

She made a dismissive sound. "I don't want to talk about their meddling. In a way, they're no different from anyone else. Everyone thinks they know what is best for us. Everyone is wrong. We know what is best for us."

Tupperman watched her for a moment, wondering how angels had meddled in her plans, beyond the story she'd already told him. "Are they responsible for the loss you mourn?" She glanced at him in confusion. "You are dressed all in black."

Kara averted her gaze and fell silent.

Tupperman knew he should accept the chance to end their conversation, even if it condemned them to mutual silence for their journey. But he couldn't do it. Kara looked so stricken that he wished he could mend whatever had been destroyed in her life. A few words of conversation seemed a small concession.

"Maybe the angels are trying to atone for their deed," he suggested.

Kara gave a short laugh. "Then they need to try harder." She straightened, then reached out and put her hand on his thigh again. "But you, Tupperman, you've already given me hope for the future."

Tupperman was so aware of the weight of her hand on his leg

that he could hardly summon a coherent thought. "How?"

"By having green eyes and admitting to the possibility of finding me attractive. It is better news than I've had in a while. May I speak bluntly?"

Tupperman nodded, convinced that she was incapable of doing otherwise.

Kara leaned closer, her breast touching his arm. Her voice dropped to a murmur. "We could make a child, Tupperman." Her eyes shone as she made this outrageous yet appealing suggestion. "We could make a prophecy come true. My mother also said that hope has the greatest power of all."

"Hope. Why? Who would have hope?"

"My people." She slid her hand down his leg, her gaze dropping to his mouth. "Would making a child be so arduous a task?" Her hand moved up his thigh then, thrilling him with its slow progress.

Awakening him to new possibilities.

Tempting him.

"No, not at all," Tupperman admitted, without having any intention of doing so. Kara held his gaze, then looked at his mouth again. A small smile curved her lips and Tupperman couldn't look away. He was beguiled.

He wasn't surprised when she reached up and touched his jaw with her free hand, though the feel of her fingertips against his skin sent a jolt through him. This was a woman who would defy expectations, push the odds, always surprise him.

Even though he feared it was a mistake, he was powerless to turn away.

When she slid her finger across his bottom lip, Tupperman had to close his eyes against the rising tide of desire.

And the darkness reminded him of Lucifer.

The fallen angel who routinely tempted and corrupted his fellows.

The demon whose province was temptations of the flesh.

Tupperman lunged to his feet and stepped over Kara, marching with purpose down the car. There had to be a reservations computer in the next car. There had to be a way to get his seat reassigned. There had to be a way to keep himself from making a mistake.

His heart thundered the entire way, and his lips burned with the promise of what he had denied himself.

Was he wise?

Or a fool?

Tupperman had a laze.

He'd come through all the security checks and baggage inspections, yet he was carrying a laze. Kara had felt its distinctive shape when she'd leaned against him, hoping for a kiss.

That could only mean that he was licensed to carry it.

She bit her lip and considered that inescapable truth.

Worse, he was wearing a pseudoskin. She'd glimpsed the cuff of it protruding from his sleeve the second time he'd taken off his glove. Those suits followed the contours of the body, fitting like a second skin, and were made in layers of polymer with lead mesh embedded. They offered protection to the wearer from the effects of radiation in hot zones, but were very expensive. The best ones were custom-made to fit perfectly. Most citizens didn't have the means to buy such a wardrobe item. Most didn't really have the need for one, either, as people avoided the hot zones of the old cities.

But Tupperman was wearing one, hidden under his clothes.

Yet he wasn't sitting in the first class compartment. He couldn't be some wealthy man with a taste for expensive equipment—never mind the laze.

Then who was he? A cop?

One of the government's security corps?

She shook her head in dismay. He might as well be an angel.

His hasty departure gave Kara a moment to think and perhaps an opportunity to save herself from an impetuous decision. She forced herself to think of practicalities, rather than the kiss she'd been denied. Tupperman was still handsome, even more attractive now that she'd talked to him, but his equipment suggested he had secrets.

Not that Kara didn't have a few of her own.

On the one hand, the pseudoskin explained his toned physique. The extra weight of the embedded lead ensured that anyone who regularly wore one was strong and fit. Tupperman was lean and powerful—even in a seated position, Kara could see that he was all muscle. He didn't just own a pseudoskin: he wore it routinely.

A laze and a pseudoskin meant he probably was a cop, and that he was headed for trouble in a hot zone. But a cop from the east would have no jurisdiction in the west, unless he was federal. That wasn't reassuring. Also, there was no hot zone in Fresno.

Where was he really going?

And why?

Kara could still see him in her mind's eye. She had a good memory and could carry an image for years, studying it to find more detail. She did that now, seeking some critical clue that she'd missed. Tupperman wore tall black boots, much like her own, dark trousers and a jacket of deep green that was a few years out of style. All the same, it looked as if it had never been worn, which added to her sense that he was pretending to be other than he was. His cravat was too perfectly tied and crisp to be a garment he wore habitually. There was a self-consciousness in the knot, as if he'd done it repeatedly to get it right. There was a faint whiff of smoke to him, as if the memory of a fire clung to his jacket.

Maybe he'd bought his clothing used.

But those eyes. They were relentless, riveting, piercing. Intelligent. Calculating. Observant.

Sexy.

Tupperman was definitely flesh and blood. He was a man, and one with a heat in his gaze that made Kara aware she was a woman. He was handsome enough to remind her that Derek had been dead for six years, to make her yearn for one pleasure that had vanished from her life long before that.

She remembered how steady Tupperman's gaze was, how reluctantly he smiled. He was a man who had not always had things to smile about, Kara was sure of it, and she was tempted to change that situation for him. The more she thought about it, the more she felt awakened and excited. The making of a child could be a wondrous event with a man like Tupperman.

But that laze. Tupperman carried his laze on the left, just below his heart, which meant he was right-handed and liked to be able to grab it quickly. A decisive man then, and one inclined to action. She wasn't afraid of the fact that he was armed, because Tupperman had the cool composure characteristic of those who used firearms responsibly.

Kara had known enough of the opposite kind to recognize the

difference.

Tupperman had also spoken to her as if she were his equal. That must be why she was determined to think well of him. That hadn't been a common occurrence of late, and not just with the Watchful Host. With her ancestry, she might as well have been a shade in the Republic. She instinctively liked Tupperman for that.

Still, she needed to know more about him before she made a choice.

His backpack remained on the floor in front of his seat.

He had departed so abruptly that he must have forgotten it. Kara didn't imagine that Tupperman forgot details very often and didn't believe he would do it again. Who knew how long he would be gone?

When opportunity knocked, Kara always answered. She studied the bag, memorizing its position, then bent down and opened it. She wasn't sure what she was looking for, but she guessed that she'd know when she found it.

She did: Tupperman had a map folded open to the site of the Trinity detonation.

The Eye of Glass.

Her home.

The hair prickled on the back of Kara's neck. It couldn't be a coincidence. Why was he really going west?

She wasn't going to spend hours seated beside him on this train without finding out.

III

There was nothing worse, in Tupperman's estimation, than arguing with a computer.

The problem was simple: he had to change seats. Immediately. Kara troubled him. She intrigued him. All of this could only distract him from his earthly quest, whatever it might prove to be. The train was his opportunity to rest and ensure he was at his best.

There was a reservation computer on every train, and on this train, it was two cars back from his own. Tupperman realized too late that he'd left his bag at his seat, but there was no line at the display and he didn't want to take the time to retrieve the bag.

This should only take a moment.

Tupperman typed in his request, and the computer insisted he could not change his seat assignment. It declared that the train was at full capacity, which—to its credit—appeared to be true.

He swore under his breath and made another request.

A man chuckled.

Tupperman glanced over his shoulder to find a short man with grey hair had come to stand behind him, apparently also waiting to use the computer. His nose had a distinctive hook to it, his eyes were dark and his skin was tanned.

"Nothing like a train whore, is there?" that man said amiably. Tupperman was surprised by the comment, but the man jerked his head toward Tupperman's seat and Kara. How had he seen her? Tupperman hadn't noticed this man walk past them. "A man's got no choice but to move when one tries to latch on."

Tupperman didn't reply but returned his attention to his request. A train whore? It was true that Kara's manner was bold, but he didn't believe she was a prostitute.

Even if she had removed her gloves.

Even if she had put her hand on his thigh.

Even if she had propositioned him.

Tupperman typed more quickly.

The man continued to talk. "I halfway think the train service works with them. No sooner does one get you cornered than the computer insists you can't change seats."

"I don't think she's a train whore," Tupperman said tightly.

The man laughed, as if he thought Tupperman naive. "Just because she didn't set the price doesn't mean she's not in the profession." Tupperman glanced back in time to see the man smile. "The world's oldest profession."

The computer meanwhile declined the request again, then sternly reminded Tupperman of the fee that could be levied against those who were not found in their assigned seats with a paid ticket in the case of random spot-checks.

In some fundamental ways, the Republic had not changed at all.

Tupperman sighed, realizing he'd have to make the best of it or get off the train. He stepped back to consider his choices and gestured to the computer, inviting the other man to take his turn.

He stared out the window as the man pushed credits into the slot, evidently adding another leg to his journey.

How would he get to New Mexico if he got off the train here? No, he had to stay on board. The dining car, he noted, was closed for the night, so he couldn't evade Kara there.

Maybe Kara would sleep most of the way. Maybe if he denied her request to make a child, she'd turn her attentions to another green-eyed man.

The prospect was annoying, proof positive that he had to move.

He drummed his fingers on the sill of the window, watching the land speed past. They would reach Charleston in an hour or so. The high-speed train would take less than twenty-four hours to reach Albuquerque. Surely he could evade one woman's questions for that long?

"Good luck," the other man said amiably. "No offense, but I'm betting on the whore. A decent man has no chance against one of them." He grinned, then sauntered down the car, his business concluded. He took a seat halfway down the car between this one and Tupperman's and bent to talk to his companion.

This was ridiculous. One woman shouldn't be able to distract him so much. Tupperman made his peace with the situation and told himself to focus on how he'd escape her attention when they both deboarded in Albuquerque.

Annoyed, he strode back through the train.

He was shocked to find the map from his backpack spread across his seat, his destination on top. His heart stopped cold.

There was no doubt who had opened his bag, for Kara's eyes were glittering with anger. "Liar," she said softly. "You're not going to Fresno at all."

Once again, Tupperman was startled by how direct Kara was. He stifled his irritation and stepped around her, snatching his map and folding it up. He was typically a man who was in complete control of his emotions and his situation, but since he had met Kara, he'd been aroused and felt volatile. He didn't much like the change.

On the other hand, she was provocative and intriguing—more intriguing than any other mortal he'd met.

He took his seat in bad temper and pushed the map back into his backpack. "Find anything else of interest in my belongings?"

"I didn't look past the map. It was interesting enough."

"Why?"

"Because it's always interesting when people lie." She repeated a long-held conviction of his own so calmly that he might have been the one speaking.

"Did your mother say that?" Tupperman spared her a glance.

She smiled. "No. She said that everyone who lies has a reason for doing so. What's yours?"

He bristled, disliking that he felt out of control of the conversation—or even himself. "I don't owe you any explanations..."

"No explanations. Just tell me what you know about the Eye of Glass."

Tupperman turned to look at her. He wasn't surprised to find her expression so serene, even when she was deliberately pushing him. It was just another of her many contrasts. "The what?"

"The Eye of Glass. Is that your real destination?"

"I don't know anything about an eye of glass."

"Then let me tell you about it." Kara stretched like a cat, as if there was nothing more natural than their discussion. If she was at ease, Tupperman was far from it.

But he was too interested in whatever she might say to interrupt.

"The Eye of Glass is a vast circle of pale green glass in the desert. When the Trinity test bomb was detonated, the heat of the explosion fused the desert into glass. Sound more familiar?"

Tupperman deliberately avoided her gaze. His fingers fell of their own accord to the piece of stone in his pocket, turning it restlessly. "What a fascinating bit of trivia."

"It's not common for people to journey across the country to see it, Tupperman. I'm intrigued that you would bother. There must be a specific reason for your journey."

Tupperman had no interest in making confessions. "My having a map of New Mexico doesn't prove that I'm not going to Fresno."

"You even wore your pseudoskin," she said softly. "All prepared for the worst in an area still contaminated by radiation."

Tupperman looked at her in alarm. "You're guessing."

"The Eye of Glass is the only remotely hot site in the vicinity. Although you don't really need a pseudoskin anymore. I've never had the luxury of owning one."

"Let's not talk about radiation theory."

"Are you a Nuclear Darwinist? Oh, I know that they've been discredited, but that doesn't mean they're gone. And they do have a vested interest in sources of radiation."

"I am not a Nuclear Darwinist." Tupperman couldn't hide his dislike of them.

Kara tipped her head to study him. "A nuclear tourist, then?"

"You're too nosy."

She smiled. "My mother said that, too."

Tupperman said nothing, merely stared out the window.

"Maybe you had a shade child."

Tupperman kept silent.

Kara leaned closer. Tupperman stole a glance at her lips, shadowed behind the veil, and felt an abrupt surge of desire. He was tempted to kiss her, as he should not have been. He thought of her fingers on his mouth, her breast against his arm, her suggestion that they conceive a child together—and couldn't think about anything else.

"I thought you might want to get some sleep," he said, his tone more brusque than he expected.

Kara wasn't visibly offended. "I might have, until I realized I was sitting next to a liar." She braced her elbow on the armrest once again and leaned her chin on her hand, fixing that dark gaze upon him. Tupperman's heart thumped. "Do you sleep well in the presence of those you can't trust?"

He laughed shortly. "You get better at it over time."

Her eyes narrowed, but Tupperman had had enough of her questions. He pulled up his collar and turned toward the darkness that rushed past the windows, then closed his eyes as if to sleep.

He would ignore her.

He would.

Even if his entire body was humming with an urgent need beyond anything he'd experienced before. Twenty-two hours, and he'd never see her again.

Those twenty-two hours would feel like eternity.

But what about the time after their ways parted? Would he ever encounter a woman so interesting again? Would he be haunted for all eternity by the opportunity he'd declined? He'd never before felt there was so much he hadn't experienced in the mortal realm, not until meeting this woman.

He felt Kara watching him. She was quiet for a mortal, surprisingly still for a woman, but he was aware of her attention. It was only when they left Charleston, over an hour later, that she finally sighed and averted her gaze. He knew when she drifted into sleep, when she surrendered the challenge of uncovering his secrets.

But he knew the reprieve wouldn't last.

He was surprised to realize how much he looked forward to their next exchange.

He turned to watch her as she slept, knowing he hadn't met such a fascinating mortal in a long, long time.

No, he *never* had.

And the notion that he should seize the opportunity to know her better only grew stronger with every passing mile.

Armand and Theodora's nest was as busy as a hive.

The space was darkened and filled with shadows, numerous people working over digital displays. Most of the juice they liberated or generated was used to run computers. Ferris had no idea how large the facility was or how many people lived in it, and he knew better than to ask. Shadowed doorways opened from the central room, undoubtedly leading to kitchens and bedrooms and other storerooms, but Ferris only looked at what he was shown. He noticed some familiar faces and nodded to a few former shades he'd met before, but mostly, he minded his own business.

That was the way of it among the Wraiths.

He'd told everything he knew to Armand and Theodora, plus everything he suspected. They'd divided up the work, assigning various lines of enquiry to different people. Ferris didn't doubt that the assignments were based on individual talents, and he trusted them to do what was right.

He was well aware of Tag on the far side of the room, although she appeared to be oblivious to everything except her own display. She was lean and almost as tall as him, as intent as he could be, but remarkably feminine. Ferris fought his curiosity about her tattoos and her attitude, knowing that time was of the essence to help Tupperman.

He was working his way through the ranks of the Watchful Host, looking for anomalies. He wasn't finding much of anything and was more than frustrated by his lack of progress. The only suite of data he could consistently access was the message hub for outside correspondence. He knew the Host had to have an internal intelligence network, and suspected that was where he'd find what he sought. He only caught glimpses of its datatrail before it disappeared again.

It could have been a live thing, like an animal that he stalked through the forest as it fled before him.

Ferris sat back and rubbed his eyes, knowing he needed another approach.

"They're only officially dead," Tag said from right beside him.

Ferris nearly jumped out of his skin. "You move quietly even for a Wraith," he complained.

Her eyes narrowed again. "And what would you know about that?"

"Enough," Ferris said flatly, noting the flare of curiosity in her eyes. They were clear blue, but filled with a suspicion that made them seem darker.

"They called you Ferris."

"Because it's my name. I assume that's why they called you Tag."

She smiled thinly. "No. It's not my name. It's the one I chose." She turned her back on him so decisively that Ferris felt dismissed. He understood that Tag, no matter how interesting he found her, wasn't interested in him. She might not be interested in anybody.

Ferris returned to the question at hand. "What do you mean, only officially dead?"

She leaned over him, tapping at the display. "They're all dead but not. Like this guy. Derek White."

Ferris frowned. Why did that name sound familiar?

He felt Armand and Theodora come to stand behind him as Tag brought up her findings on his screen. "He was a Native American rebel, shot in a protest against the police in Texas about six years ago." She pulled up an identification image of a man with silvering hair and a hooked nose, one with hostility in his eyes.

Armand indicated the screen. "Killed during a protest blaming angels for the recession in the Republic."

"Same philosophy," Theodora noted.

Tag tapped the screen again and pulled up a surveillance vid, one that featured the same man. "Yet he got on a train in New D.C. just last night."

"Good work," Theodora breathed.

"Tell me it's not Tupperman's train," Armand said, giving voice to the first thought all of them had.

"Same one," Tag said with satisfaction and Ferris felt cold.

"I don't believe in coincidence," Theodora said. "And I don't like it. Let's see where else we can find this guy."

"And any of the other not-dead members," Armand added.

Tag moved to flick her wrist and dismiss the display, but Ferris caught at her hand. The brief contact sent a thrill through him, but he hid his reaction, pointing at the screen. "Can you enlarge the image?"

She cast him a disparaging glance. "What part?"

"This guy here." Ferris exhaled and sat back after Tag did as he asked, unable to believe his eyes. "It's Captain Pierce," he said quietly.

"Who?"

Ferris was into the Watchful Host database again, pulling up Pierce's records. "Tupperman's official contact was Jackson, but Pierce always tagged along for their meetings."

"A witness?" Armand asked.

"Or security." Theodora said with a nod. "There's no Captain Pierce on the train manifest, though. He must be using an alias."

"He might not be on the train," Tag said. "He might just have been in the station." She streamed the vid-feed, and as White boarded the train, it appeared that Pierce moved away from the platform.

"He could have got on later, or at another stop," Tag murmured. "Let's check the vids."

Ferris dove back into the Watchful Host's databanks.

"What are you doing?" Tag asked with some impatience. "There's a lot of vid."

"And a lot of correspondence." Ferris was already hacking into the message archive for members of the Watchful Host. "They use a central host of servers, even for personal messages," he explained. "For security reasons."

"Also handy for hacking," Tag said. Ferris guessed that she'd seen it was the one area he'd been able to access.

"Does Pierce know Derek White?" he asked aloud, knowing none of them knew the answer yet. "Do any of the Watchful Host know him?"

"I'll check the security vids," Theodora said, then turned to Tag. "See if you can verify the names of any more not-dead members of the Brotherhood. Ferris can search the message archive for all of them."

Ferris bent over his display, sensing that they'd found the way to locate the Brotherhood. He just hoped they could sift through the high volume of data in time.

From *The New Republican Record*, November 20, 2105.

Soldier Missing in Action?

New D.C.—The New Republican Record has learned the body of one of the soldiers killed in the most recent raid of the Watchful Host was not recovered from the scene. The press office of the Watchful Host refuses to officially confirm this story, although a source within the elite corps has told our reporter that Captain Rumford's internal file indicates he is missing and presumed dead.

Rumors have been circulating that the soldier might have survived the assault and been taken captive. The Watchful Host, however, denies that any ransom demands have been made or are expected.

This most recent incident in the history of the Republic's most highly trained soldiers remains veiled in secrecy, with no details yet available as to the location of the raid or its chronology. Although the Brotherhood of Honest Laborers declares that they acted in self defense and that last week's incident was upon their stronghold, the Watchful Host has not even confirmed the identity of the targeted rebels.

The Speaker of the House today demanded an investigation into the botched operation, insisting that even the Watchful Host must be accountable to the citizens of the Republic.

Tupperman intended to remain vigilant, but the rocking motion of the shadowed train, the darkness outside the windows and the slow breathing of those around him conspired against him. He fought the urge to doze even as he realized just how exhausted he was.

The train cars were locked, the other inhabitants all asleep. Kara's head had fallen against his shoulder, her warmth pressed against his side. He felt comfortable, although still enticed by her, relaxed as he seldom was. His eyelids drifted shut even as he reasoned that a moment's rest wouldn't hurt.

And then he heard a whisper in his ear.

"Trouble in Paradise?"

That husky voice made Tupperman think of a blackness utterly devoid of light, even given the thread of humor underlying the tone.

Tupperman's eyes flew open and he looked around. The train car was exactly the same, but there was an image in the window.

One that wasn't a reflection of anything or anyone in the car.

A dark angel, who smiled in recognition, one whose body had a gleam of obsidian to it—at least where Tupperman couldn't see the shadowed countryside though him.

Lucifer! He was supposed to be vanquished, but evidently that wasn't the case.

His own reflection was that of a man asleep, and Tupperman struggled against the sense that he and Kara looked like a couple, dozing together.

He was having a vision or a dream, then.

"I'm surprised you remember Paradise," Tupperman said. "How many millennia has it been?"

"Come now." Lucifer smiled. "You can't remember the heavenly sphere with that much fondness, Turiel."

Tupperman caught his breath at the sound of his angelic name. "Don't call me that here!"

Lucifer continued as if he hadn't spoken. "After all, you chose to stay here for years instead of completing your mission and regaining your wings. Could it be that you prefer the pleasures for the flesh?" His gaze roved over Kara and his eyes widened with obvious appreciation.

"No." Tupperman spoke firmly even though he felt the back of his neck heating. Kara stirred in her sleep and placed her hand on his leg again.

Lucifer chuckled. "I see."

"You see only the wickedness you want to see."

The demon dismissed that comment with a wave of his hand. "Such a waste in New D.C. last week, don't you agree?"

So, he'd come to talk about the Watchful Host. "I'd expect you to be pleased."

"You're right," Lucifer said with glee. "More for me."

Tupperman noted the malicious gleam in Lucifer's eyes but didn't understand. "For you?"

"What do you think happens to fallen angels when they die in this realm?" Lucifer asked, expressing the concern that troubled Tupperman. "They don't get their wings back."

"No, they wouldn't."

Lucifer smiled and held up an open hand, closing it into a fist. "They become mine."

Tupperman was shocked. "They do not!"

"It's right there in the Book of Enoch. Fallen angels go to hell. Look it up."

"You're lying." It couldn't be true. All those lost commandos from the Watchful Host trapped in hell for eternity? If Tupperman had felt a sense of responsibility before, it had just multiplied a dozen times.

"But what if I'm not?" Lucifer whispered in Tupperman's ear, echoing his thoughts. "What if I'm telling you the truth and you— the angel Turiel, the so-called 'rock of God'—have condemned fallen angels to eternal torment and damnation? Tsk tsk."

Tupperman was certain he'd be sick.

"I should recruit you," Lucifer gloated. "That's very good work. Impressive for a neophyte." The demon whistled through his teeth. "Think of the future you could have. I'd put you at my right hand, place you in charge of an army of minions. We could change the world, you and I."

The idea was abhorrent. Lucifer was watching him so closely that Tupperman had to wonder whether the other angel could still read the thoughts of his fellows.

"They can't have been consigned to hell," he argued. "They can't be yours. It wouldn't be right. It wouldn't be divine justice."

"If you say so," Lucifer agreed amiably, examining his nails.

"But if that's so, then where are they?"

"The divine spark returns to the creator."

"Does it? Always?"

"Tell me you don't have them captive in your realm."

"I can tell you anything you want." Lucifer winked. "Or I can tell you the truth. Your choice."

"You're a liar, through and through. You just want another chance to manifest."

Lucifer's grin flashed. "And why not? I tell you, the opportunities are boundless. No sooner do I think the good guys have won, than humans invoke me by word and deed all over again. Look at me! I'm getting stronger by the minute, and this time I might win it all." He dropped his voice to a hiss. "Wouldn't you like to snatch back those angelic souls and set me back a bit?"

Oh, Tupperman would!

"You'd never suggest as much if you were going to give me a chance of winning."

"I knew you'd be interested," Lucifer said with confidence. Tupperman glanced up in surprise and the old demon grinned. "Oh yes, I *can* read your thoughts. Do you miss that?"

"If you were worried about losing that power, you wouldn't be so intent upon taking flesh," he muttered but Lucifer laughed.

"Do we have a deal? You were always the gallant type, Turiel."

"You haven't told me the terms."

"Simplicity itself. You know your destination. You will face me in that place, angel to demon, and fight for the souls of the fallen. Whoever is triumphant claims them all."

"Fight how?"

"However either of us chooses." Lucifer grinned again. "What do you say? Deal?"

"Deal," Tupperman agreed. This was his quest. He had no inclination to deny it. His new quest was to save these eighteen angels, though he had no idea how it would be done. He could only have been granted the task because it could be won, regardless of Lucifer's trickery.

Suddenly Lucifer's image faded and Tupperman saw his own reflection awaken and stare back with resolve. The dream was over. He was fairly sure there would be at least one trick played upon him by the Prince of Darkness, and more than one attempt to shift the result of the fight unfairly.

But it didn't matter. The angels needed his help and he had no real choice but to give it.

More, Tupperman understood now that he'd never return to New Gotham. He'd save the lost angels and possibly die in the act. Success would be enough to have his wings restored.

And if he failed, he deserved eternal torment instead.

He considered Kara as she slept beside him, and wondered what else he might accomplish in his final days in the earthly sphere.

Kara was in Derek's old red truck. Unlike so many others, he always seemed to find either canola or the credit to get it. His truck and his ability to go where he wanted when he wanted had been part of his allure. Kara, though, had come to the point of having many questions—about canola, about the supply sources, about Derek.

The truck had a jagged crack across the windshield that hadn't been there when he'd taught her to drive. It was night, near home, and the view of the stars was distorted through the crack.

Kara couldn't help staring at it. It was a potent reminder of the direction their relationship was taking. The windshield had cracked when he'd hit her the first time, slamming her head into the glass.

He'd done that months before, when she'd learned she was pregnant, and now the baby was coming.

Derek was driving, his features in silhouette. His profile was distinctive, his nose so hooked that she'd recognize it anywhere. "Middle of the fucking night," he muttered. "It figures you'd have to have the baby in the middle of the night."

Kara felt the familiar flicker of fear, the one triggered by that tone in his voice. She wanted to run and hide, to escape the man who had once charmed her, to leave him forever. But he was the father of her child, and she had come to believe his declarations that she wouldn't be able to survive alone.

A contraction ripped through her body with greater force than the ones before and she cried out in pain.

"Don't make a mess on the seat," Derek said with impatience.

"That would just be the perfect touch, if I had to spend all day cleaning up after your brat."

It wouldn't be Derek who cleaned it up, Kara knew that. He'd leave the mess until she left the hospital and demand that she clean it, as penance.

She hated him.

She was terrified of him.

She was alone except for him and uncertain what to do. He'd made her into a different person, one she barely recognized, but Kara didn't like that either. She saw with sudden clarity that it was time to reclaim herself and her life.

"It's not as if I can control it," Kara snapped, just as she had on that first night.

Derek's nostrils flared at her tone and he cast her a quick glance, noting the change in her manner. She was sure that if he hadn't been driving, he would have raised his hand. But he was driving and she'd had enough. "Why did you have to get pregnant anyway?"

"I didn't do it alone!"

"No, you didn't." Derek's lips tightened and she knew he would say something ugly, but another contraction coursed through her body. She moaned and tried to clench her muscles, although she knew she couldn't control the breaking of her water. She gripped the door handle and eyed the approaching lights of the hospital.

Derek swore and pushed the accelerator to the floor.

"I should kick you out of my truck, you worthless bitch," he muttered. "I should let your bastard child rip you open and leave you bleeding in the dirt. Food for the vultures, just like you deserve."

Kara believed he would do it, but she wouldn't back down. "I've told you a thousand times. It's not another man's child. It's yours."

He snorted. "That's what you say." He flicked her a hot look. "The baby had better be perfect. No mutations from you hanging around the Eye of Glass."

"I went because my mother used to go..."

"Maybe that's what's wrong with you. Maybe she went there when she was pregnant, and that's why you're so worthless."

They entered town, driving too fast but Kara just hung on. Her body contracted again, the pain rippling through her body and obliterating all other concerns. There was only the child. Only this moment.

And a vision of what her future would be if she stayed with Derek.

If. Her old confidence rose within her once more.

"Your brat better not have green eyes," Derek growled.

"How could that happen? For the hundredth time, it's your baby, Derek..."

"Don't lie to me!" He raised his hand and Kara flinched.

But she didn't back down this time.

"That's it!" she cried. "I'm not going home with you! That's it. We're done."

"We're done when I say we're done," he snarled and swung at her, turning his attention away from the road.

Kara saw the car pull out of the side street. She saw the shadow of Derek's hand, the hatred in his expression. She knew the truck was moving too fast. She saw the horrified look on the other driver's face, then the next contraction came with savage force. Events unfolded in slow motion, as if the crash were inevitable.

"No!" Kara screamed. "My baby!" Derek hit her across the face. There was a scream and the sound of the crash...

Suddenly, Kara felt strong hands gripping her upper arms. She was shaken hard as a man called her name, his voice pulling her back to reality.

Just as someone might haul a drowning person from the water.

Kara took a shuddering breath and opened her eyes.

Tupperman was leaning over her, his expression filled with concern. "Kara!" he whispered urgently. Her own hands were locked over his, clutching him convulsively. He gave her a shake as she stared at him, not comprehending his presence for a moment. Where was the truck? The hospital?

Her baby?

"It's all right." He lifted one brow. "You're on the train. Remember?"

She did remember although she had to struggle against her tears. The nightmare had undermined her composure, leaving her with the sense that she was revealed to Tupperman's sharp gaze. It was tempting to lean on him, as he seemed so reliable and trustworthy.

But Kara swallowed, then turned away from whatever solace he might offer.

"I think you were having a dream." He studied her, then released her arms. "Not a good one."

"No. Not a good one." Kara took a shaky breath.

The sky was lightening. It was close to dawn. She was in the train, headed home, not in the truck headed to the hospital. She blinked back her tears and passed a hand over her face, hoping Tupperman hadn't noticed them.

She was sure he had.

"Are you all right?" he asked more quietly.

"Fine," she said with a grateful smile. "I hope I didn't wake you up. Where are we?"

"Coming into St. Louis. You slept a while."

Kara nodded. She could believe it. She hadn't slept well in the city. There was no space, no wind, no soil. The city had churned with restless energy and the sense of too many people pressed around her. It had been a turmoil of sensation and noise, none of it welcome.

But she had slept beside Tupperman.

Because she felt safe beside him, despite his many secrets.

She looked at him again, wondering what it was about him that so prompted her trust. She hadn't trusted any man in years, not since Derek, and she hadn't planned to trust Tupperman. She'd hoped to charm him, maybe conceive a child with his help, but that was a far cry from trust. He was looking out the window again, being diplomatic, but she had to know that her instincts were right.

"Have you ever hit a woman?" Kara asked, not bothering to prepare him for the question. She wanted to see his reaction when he had no warning.

Tupperman was visibly shocked, which was all the answer she needed. "Is that what you were dreaming about?"

Kara nodded. "My last night with my husband."

Tupperman's expression was wary. "But you talked about a

baby.”

“I was in labor. He was sure it would have green eyes.”

Tupperman frowned. “But you said your husband had dark eyes.”

“He did. He thought I would be more interested in fulfilling my mother’s prophecy than in being faithful to him.” She caught his questioning glance. “It was his child. My daughter had brown eyes.” Her tears rose again and she had to look down at her hands as the silence stretched between them. Her ovaries, swollen with possibilities, throbbed. The countryside swept past them in a blur, the dim security lighting in the train car giving it an air of false intimacy.

Never mind Tupperman’s steady gaze.

Hope might be potent, but sometimes it seemed crazy.

“Had,” Tupperman echoed softly and Kara almost smiled that he hadn’t missed that detail. He was observant.

If he was a cop, he was probably a good one.

“Had,” she agreed.

There was silence between them for a few moments, and she knew he was considering what she had told him. She wondered what he would do or say, and found herself prepared to wait to find out.

“I’m confused,” Tupperman admitted finally, stretching out his legs to cross them at the ankles. Kara watched his movement, noting again his easy grace. That he moved slowly calmed her in a way she didn’t expect. “You seem to be very direct and outspoken, the kind of woman who isn’t easily intimidated. Why would you marry a man who hit you?”

“I didn’t.” Kara sighed, remembering her own foolishness. “I married a man who was handsome and charming, if a little rebellious. He was older and mysterious. I was young and didn’t look beyond the adventure of being with him.” She almost laughed. “My mother hated him, which was a good endorsement in that phase of my life.”

“He wasn’t the only rebellious one , then?”

She heard the smile in Tupperman’s voice and shook her head. “No. You see, I was tired of being a disappointment. My mother was a seer and the gift is supposed to pass through the female line in our family. I didn’t have it. I think she believed for a long time that I had it, but wasn't confiding in her."

"A difficult relationship?"

"Two headstrong and outspoken women. Now, I understand that we were very similar. I think I infuriated her."

Tupperman chuckled, as if unwillingly.

Kara looked up to find his gaze warm.

"I can't imagine why," he said, with the air of a man who thought just the opposite.

Kara smiled at his teasing.

"Did she infuriate you?"

"Oh yes." Kara sobered. "And I was tired of being a failure in her eyes, so when Derek proposed and my mother opposed it, I chose him. It was after we were married that he hit me." She swallowed. "After I was pregnant." She considered the timing with the distance of years. "After I had nowhere to go and no one to turn to."

"A coincidence?"

Kara exhaled. "Probably not."

"Your mother wouldn't have welcomed you back?"

"She died, right after I ran away with Derek. I always wondered whether my choice killed her." Kara studied her hands. "I abandoned her, and it was only when it was far too late that I realized my mistake."

"Everyone makes mistakes."

"If not such spectacular ones."

Tupperman stared out the window, so obviously giving her time to compose herself that Kara's heart warmed to him all the more.

"So, what happened to the gift? The one that should run in your family?"

"My daughter had it," Kara said with pride.

"What was her name?" He was clearly interested.

"Dionta. She was the light of my life. Her gift was clear even before she could talk. She'd look to the door five minutes before anyone arrived. Little things like that. And even in baby talk, she said the most remarkable things." Struck by her own use of the past tense, Kara dropped her gaze, her heart aching with grief all over again.

"Was your husband pleased that her eyes were brown?"

Kara shook her head. "He never saw her. He was going to hit me when I was in labor. I had decided to leave him and that was the wrong answer. Because he was violent, he wasn't allowed to see me or the baby."

"That could have been hard for him."

"I was told that he never even tried to see either of us." Kara heaved a sigh. "I heard months later he'd been killed, resisting arrest in Dallas."

That wasn't the end of the story, but Kara ran out of the need to confess. She was thinking of her small, sweet daughter, the soft smell of her, the way she smiled, the way she came for a cuddle, the way her eyes lit with anticipation when she sensed a surprise. She felt Tupperman watching her, but couldn't look up, couldn't bear to see the compassion in his expression that she knew would be there.

"What happened to your daughter, Kara?" he asked quietly.

"She died." Kara lifted her head, blinking back her tears as she reached for her bag. "Are there restrooms in this car?"

IV

Tag didn't trust her own reaction.

Ferris was an outsider. He was a stranger and a new arrival. She'd learned young that visitors never brought anything good with them, and that outsiders weren't to be trusted. Worse, he'd smelled like forest and earth when she'd opened the door, like the outdoors and the open fields. Tag stifled a shudder. She hated the wilderness. She hated the unpredictability of the natural world, of animals and even of other people. Emotions and instincts were unreliable and inconsistent.

Just look at her now, intrigued by a guy who couldn't be more wrong for her. It was irrational to the point of being stupid. He was just new, different. If she'd met him in a crowd, he wouldn't have been interesting.

It was his name that got her. Ferris. When she was young, Tag had wanted a friend more than anything in the world. She hadn't had one. Even in the slave dens, she'd been alone. The story of the Oracle Delilah and her loyal friend Ferris had been a potent one for Tag, when she'd first heard it. Her life would have been so much different with such a friend.

So much better.

But this guy wasn't that Ferris. He had no scars. He was good-looking and healthy. He knew nothing about shades and netherzones, about solitude and pain. Who knew how he knew Theodora. Maybe he'd been a customer of the Wraiths, buying whatever he wanted for easy cred. He was exactly the kind of person Tag most disliked—yet she was stupidly, irrationally, interested in him.

She was losing her edge.

Only machines were reliable, machines that were on or off, doing what they had been designed to do, over and over and over again without variation.

On the other hand, Ferris had improved from that first impression. He'd eaten and washed before coming into the main research room, and didn't smell so wild anymore. He smelled like soap and warmth and a little bit like the vegetable soup that was always available in the kitchen of Theodora's sanctuary.

It was more than that, though. Tag liked how intent he was, how agile his fingers were, how quickly he made connections. His mind didn't seem to be that different from her own, another finely honed machine that was good at what it did.

Too bad he was a norm. She'd seen his grimace when he'd noticed her scarred skin, and she knew what that meant. He had no experience with imperfection.

Never mind suffering.

Tag had found six members of the Brotherhood who were only dead officially, all of whom had been vocal in their dislike of angels in their recorded lives. She'd passed the names to Ferris as they were confirmed, and he'd been looking for hints that members of the Watchful Host might have known one or several of these individuals. She hadn't found anything unusual associated with the other names, which didn't mean their files hadn't been modified, but might only mean that the Wraiths had done a better job of covering their tracks.

Theodora had noted that they might have been paid more and moved all the names into Ferris' search protocol.

Now they were all sifting through messages. Ferris had cast his net wide, separating out even messages from senders with the same initials as any of the brotherhood members, a tactic Tag thought clever. Tag had further sorted them by frequency and volume, under the assumption that contact would have been limited to a dangerous source. There were still thousands of messages.

"The dates," Tag said suddenly, sitting up straight.

"What dates?" Armand asked.

Ferris's eyes lit. He bent over the display, refining his search routine again. "The dates the commandos were killed," he muttered. "Let's try 48 hours before." He tapped and the utility sifted, then Tag smiled at her new display.

"Message to D.W.," she said. "On the 11th."

"Two days before that last fatal raid," Armand said, coming to stand behind her.

"It's nonsense," Tag said, scanning the message.

"It's in code," Theodora guessed. "Pass it to me." She began to work on the encryption, as she was the fastest with such tasks.

"Two more here," Tag said with satisfaction. "All from the same member of the Watchful Host."

"Pierce?" Ferris asked.

"It looks like it." Tag smiled. "But none of them were sent from his personal devices."

Armand leaned over her shoulder. "Public readers, in the netherzones."

"Where?" Ferris asked. "We'll check surveillance and security vids for the times and locations."

"There's no surveillance in those zones," Tag protested.

"Not officially. Every bar owner runs his own, though, and a lot of them use the same security firm." He spoke absently, assuming she'd follow his logic. "It's Safe-T-Vue in New Gotham, and yes, they're popular in New D.C., too." He glanced up at her, his gaze bright. "I'm in. Give me a location and time."

Tag smiled, impressed, and watched him blink in surprise.

Then she caught herself, realizing how dumb she'd been, and turned back to her work.

She told herself to hope that Ferris didn't stay long.

As Kara watched, Tupperman settled back, his expression watchful. He pointed to the front of the car. Kara grabbed her bag and headed that way, her heart racing. She locked the cubicle door behind herself, despising the stench of urine and city filth. She wanted to be home with a vehemence that shook her.

Why had she told Tupperman so much? She never confided so much of her story in anyone. Just because he was a good listener didn't mean she had to tell him all of her secrets. He must think her an idiot.

Kara closed her eyes, hoping he didn't think she was pathetic, stupid, or worse.

She considered her reflection, not really surprised to find that she looked disheveled and a little bit haunted. Jumpy. Not exactly alluring. If she wasn't going to be a failure, she had to pull herself together and seduce Tupperman. It was the only goal she had even a remote chance of accomplishing before arriving home.

She tugged off her hat and veil, impatient with it.

How dare Derek haunt her now?

It would be like Derek to try to poison something she enjoyed, like this conversation with Tupperman. It would be like him to ensure she didn't forget any shortcomings or failures. If the dead had any powers at all, she could believe that Derek would deliberately try to unsettle her in this moment.

Kara wished Derek would leave her alone. He was dead and good riddance. She wasn't the weak young woman who had married him anymore. She wasn't going to change for a man ever again, and she wasn't going to forget who she was. She might not have the Sight, but she would have that green-eyed child. She would fulfill her mother's prophecy and achieve *something* on this trip.

Maybe she'd even banish Derek's ghost forever.

Impatient with herself, Kara brushed her hair and redid the twist. She jammed her hat and veil into her bag, to hell with convention, then picked up her bag. She unlocked the door and immediately saw a piece of paper on the opposite wall, at eye level.

A note was written on it in letters too large to miss.

Kara—he is one of them. Watch his back.

A note for her.

Against every expectation.

Kara looked up and down the train car, but couldn't see anyone out of their seat. There was no one walking down the central aisle, and dozens of strangers dozed in their seats. The next car similarly had an empty aisle and the lights were turned down low there.

Whoever had given her the message had effectively

disappeared.

The missive was tucked into a seam on the opposite wall and Kara easily lifted it away. She fingered it with curiosity.

It was paper, a substance rarely seen in the Republic. There were few trees left to pulp to make paper, and faux-paper required too much fuel to manufacture at a reasonable cost. Since the destruction of the palm computers, people had scrounged bits of old paper from archives and used it for messages. Libraries had been torn to shreds. Occasionally, one even saw paper money used for messages, since it had no value as currency any more. Kara had never seen a piece of paper that had been used less than a dozen times, and this one was no exception.

It had been torn out of a printed book. Kara had only seen a whole book once, but she recognized the layout of a page. There were two columns of type on each side and the paper was thin. This sheet had notes written in the margins, all of which had been erased except the one she'd just read. That line looked to have been written in charcoal.

Obviously it was intended for her, and just as obviously, it was a reference to Tupperman. He was one of whom? She puzzled over the second sentence until she gasped in understanding.

The fallen angels had scars on their backs from the removal of their wings.

Could it be true?

Could he be one of the Watchful Host?

She thought about the laze and the pseudoskin, remembered her own suspicions that he might work for the Republic, and her heart chilled.

Were the Watchful Host following her? They had banned her from the reception room of the Oracle's official residence. They'd ensured she never had an audience with the Oracle, and Kara doubted that woman even knew she'd been there. Were the Watchful Host in league with the Republic, determined to marginalize her people even more?

Was Tupperman's presence really a coincidence?

If he was one of the Watchful Host, it was no wonder Tupperman was evasive about the reasons for his trip. That might explain his destination, too. Kara hated having doubts about him, but the questions were inescapable.

Kara folded the note carefully and put it in her pocket, then headed back to her seat, filled with new purpose.

Tupperman was going to tell her the truth, and he was going to do it now.

Tupperman had been shaken by Kara's dream. She had been so vulnerable and so upset. It was a complete contrast to her earlier confidence.

That only made him wonder if the dream had been faked.

But why? Why would she seek his compassion?

He believed that her distress had been genuine. Her obvious fear for the baby tore at his heart. Her blunt statement that her husband had beaten her opened Tupperman's eyes to a world he knew about, but had never personally encountered before.

Much like the way she had spoken of the treatment of her people.

And the baby had died. Her grief in that was clear.

No wonder Kara wanted to have another child.

The incredible thing was that Tupperman had the power to heal at least some of her emotional wounds. He looked out the window, wondering if he was rationalizing his desire. They could both have what they wanted. She could conceive, possibly, and fulfill her mother's prophecy—and even if the baby didn't have green eyes, its presence might make the loss of her first child less painful to bear. It was possible, after all, that one intimate encounter could diminish his fascination with her.

The intimacy alone might be a balm to her. He would never strike her—or any woman. He would never take his own pleasure first, or at the expense of hers. He could potentially repair her expectations, make her believe in goodness again.

And afterward, he would be able to immerse himself fully in his own mission.

He would risk very little and possibly learn a great deal. It would be a compassionate and good choice. His conclusion had all the neatness of a rationalization, but it was one he wanted very much to pursue.

Tupperman glanced up at Kara's return, knowing he shouldn't

have been surprised to see the determination back in her expression. He also shouldn't have been startled that she had discarded her hat and veil, nor that she was so lovely. The matron across the aisle, however, caught her breath in a sharp hiss of disapproval.

Kara ignored the censure. She sat down, dropped her bag between her feet and looked Tupperman in the eye. Her expression was challenging. "Why is my seat assignment next to yours?" Before he could speak, she shoved a piece of paper at him. "Is this true?"

Tupperman read the message quickly and understood it immediately. Panic made him glance down the length of the car. "Who gave this to you?"

"I don't know. It was left where I would see it."

Tupperman considered that. Was she deceiving him? She was so direct, he had an overwhelming sense that she was incapable of lying outright. Who had walked the length of the car while she'd been in the lavatory? There had been several people, but Tupperman had been looking out the window at the passing countryside, lost in his thoughts.

Distracted by Kara.

He stole a glance at her, jumping when he found her gaze fixed on him.

"Well?" she prompted.

"What do you think?" he asked with care.

She smiled tightly, and no warmth reached her eyes. "I'd like to see your back. I'd like to know why you're going to the Eye of Glass. And I'd like to know who you really are."

"Not all wishes come true."

She laughed unexpectedly. "No. How about one of three?"

"While you tell me nothing of your recent history," Tupperman countered with a scoff, surprised to realize he was enjoying their exchange again. "No deal."

She sat back with a smile. "All right. Ask me a question."

"Why did you go east?"

Kara didn't hesitate to reply, which enforced Tupperman's sense that she was telling the truth. "I wanted to talk to the Oracle, but the angels kept me away from her."

"Not the angels," Tupperman corrected automatically. "The Watchful Host."

"Right." She eyed him for a moment and he knew he should have kept silent. "The *fallen* angels. The ones who have shed their wings and taken flesh supposedly to help humanity. The ones who have scars on their backs." She held his gaze but Tupperman simply looked back at her.

After the angels had descended that last time and Tupperman had chosen to stay, he'd decided to echo his choice in his body. He'd seen the angels remove Rafe's scars, silencing any rumor about the Oracle's Consort, and been inspired by his choice. Tupperman had had the scars on his back removed, because it was finally possible to do as much without the risk that the mortal surgeon would report him to the authorities as a shade. He'd thought then that it was a commitment to this sphere, a sign of his intent that he would appear in all ways like a mortal man, even to understand what it was to be one. Now he was glad.

His unscarred back could win her trust.

And what would follow that? His pulse quickened at the possibilities.

Meanwhile, her eyes narrowed. "I thought the angels would count us as humans, but just like the Republic, they don't."

"You can't know that..."

"You want to defend the angels? That's a serious long shot, Tupperman. Maybe you *are* one of them." Her tone hinted that she didn't believe it. "Maybe that's why you take their side."

"Is that what you think?"

"I think someone wants me to believe that you are one, and I have to wonder why." She smiled. "Either way, I want to know who you are."

"What if we made a trade?" The question was out before he could stop it. Tupperman's gaze dropped to her lips and Kara smiled.

"What kind of trade?"

"You tell me the whole story of why you went east. Then I'll show you my back."

Her eyes narrowed. "That seems a little light on your end of the bargain."

"If you like what you see, we could work on fulfilling that prophecy."

Kara's smile was so luminous that Tupperman blinked. "And

what recourse do I have if you're just leading me on? What if you listen, then refuse to show me your back."

"No." Tupperman was firm. "I'll keep the bargain."

"Regardless of what I tell you?"

"Regardless."

Their gazes locked for a taut moment and Tupperman watched a flush stain her cheeks. He saw that she had no mark on the back of her neck, no blemish where an identity bead had been destroyed.

No, she said her people had been given numbers. It was reprehensible, a glimpse into another part of the mortal realm he'd never known about. He wondered if she had a tattoo, like a shade. He wanted to see her nude, to see the splendor of her body, and not just to check for tattoos.

He wanted to admire her. He wanted to give her pleasure. He wanted to show her that a man could treat her with honor. He wanted to restore her belief in goodness.

He wanted to leave one small mark that he had walked the earth and left it better than it would have been without him. Whether he won or lost Lucifer's challenge, there would have been a point to his existence here.

As these thoughts flew though his mind, Kara studied him. The air heated between them. There was appreciation in her gaze, an appreciation that made Tupperman realize all he'd ignored in this realm. He recognized that he was unlikely to survive his mission, and while he'd accepted that possibility earlier, Kara's presence— and the response she provoked in him—made him aware that he might have missed out on one particular human experience.

But now he had the chance.

Kara shook her head in wonder. "Who would have guessed I'd meet a man of honor on the train?" she murmured. She shook a finger at him, her eyes dancing. "Don't disappoint me, Tupperman, by breaking your word. I'm ready for the novelty of a man keeping a promise."

"You mean I could restore your faith?"

"Something like that."

"Who could ask for more?" Tupperman offered his hand. "Deal."

Kara took his hand in hers and he was struck by the softness of her skin. She leaned closer, the light in her eyes so warm and welcoming that Tupperman's mouth went dry. "It's the kind of deal we should seal with a kiss."

"Why?" Tupperman asked, even though he agreed.

"Because you can learn as much about a man from his deeds than his words, maybe more." Her gaze fell to his mouth. "And a kiss is the most telling deed of all."

"Did your mother say that?"

She chuckled in turn. "Maybe she should have."

Tupperman smiled. Kara was so easy to like, with her direct manner and her ready sense of humor, yet mysterious, too. He didn't know what she would say next, much less what she'd do, and it was all too easy to imagine spending years in her company, just to find out. She was seductive and forthright, strong and wounded.

Her smile faded as she watched him, then her lips parted in invitation. She leaned closer and Tupperman bent his head. He closed his mouth over hers, gently at first, then deepened his kiss as she welcomed his touch. She was choosing to trust him, despite her past experience.

And Tupperman wouldn't disappoint her. His free hand rose to her jaw, then slid into the dark silk of her hair. He pulled her closer, hungry for more, never wanting the kiss to stop.

Tupperman's kiss was heavenly.

Kara was utterly seduced by it. He managed to both ask permission and demand more simultaneously. He coaxed her trust and encouraged her surrender, persuading her with one kiss that he was as different from Derek as a man could be.

Kara found herself ready to yield to temptation. Her eyes were closed, his mouth warm on her own, and she sighed when his fingers locked around her nape. Tupperman pulled her closer and slanted his mouth over hers, demanding more. Kara gave it. She mirrored his pose, letting her hand slide around his neck to pull him even closer. Their shoulders collided as he kissed her more deeply.

It was a kiss that should have lasted forever, one that should have led straight to bed. She was warm and languid and filled with a rush of desire beyond any she could remember.

With just one kiss.

He lifted his lips from hers and she saw him catch his breath, saw his gaze drop to her mouth. His fingertip slid across her bottom lip and she saw a kind of wonder in his eyes. Then he smiled at her, a smile that was more heated than any yet. "You're first," he reminded her gently.

Kara didn't move away. She kept her shoulder and upper arm pressed against him, let her thigh lean against the muscled strength of his. Tupperman didn't move away. His hand, in fact, landed on her knee, a gesture that was both exciting and reassuring. Proprietary.

She would have voted on him being a mortal man, if she'd had to decide in that moment. Angels were said to be unaware of physical pleasure, and she had an idea that the fallen angels were lusty samplers of the pleasures of the flesh. Tupperman was a gentleman, one filled with quiet but very human strength.

They had an agreement.

And she had to fulfill her part of it first.

Kara exhaled to compose herself, her gaze drifting to the extinguished vid at the front of the car. She felt Tupperman watching her and wondered whether he would guess what parts of the story she omitted. She already realized that he could manage information and felt a commonality with him in that.

"My people place great faith in visions and prophecies," she began. "My mother was a seer and she made many such predictions. Not me, though. As I said, the family talent skipped me."

Tupperman looked as if he intended to ask a question, but thought the better of it after seeing her expression. A man of discretion, then, too. Kara liked that.

But what should she share? How much?

There was no short version of the story. She would have to start at the beginning.

"Uh oh," Ferris said.

Tag was on her feet and by his side in a heartbeat. He looked so troubled that she knew it couldn't be good news. The guy was an open book, another sign that he'd lived on the easy side of the

Republic.

On his display was a request from the Watchful Host for law officials in Amarillo, Texas, to intercept the west-bound express train and arrest Tupperman. They were charging him with the murder of the commando who had gone missing at the previous week's raid. It had just been issued from the main office of the Host.

"Did he do it?" she asked and earned herself a scornful glance from Ferris.

"They're closing the trap," he said flatly. "They've set him up. How much you want to bet he doesn't survive the arrest?"

"They want him that badly?"

His sidelong glance was scornful.

"Do you know that, or do you just believe it?" she asked with disdain.

"Both." He spoke with a conviction that startled Tag.

She leaned over the display beside him, even as the others in the datahub gathered around them, and challenged him. "Okay, prove it. Find the evidence? There has to be evidence before they can issue a warrant for arrest, and you're in their system."

Ferris was already searching their network. By the time Tag had asked, the warrant was filling the display

"Emergency crews responded to a fire alarm at an apartment last night, and arrived to find the unit virtually destroyed," Ferris read. "It was rented to Tupperman. The police were contacted when evidence of foul play was discovered in the wreckage." He swallowed and sat back. "The spilled blood was matched to that of the missing commando from last week's raid."

"And Tupperman's departure now looks like flight from the scene of the crime," Theodora contributed with a shake of her head.

"But why did they identify the remains from the blood sample?" Armand asked. "Wasn't the body there?"

Tag watched Ferris scan the report. "No," he said.

"Then where is it?" Tag asked. A shiver rolled down her spine, because she could think of only one way whoever was framing Tupperman could make his situation worse.

Ferris looked at her, his eyes wide. "On the train," he whispered and she nodded.

"Can we warn him?" Armand asked.

Ferris shrugged, his gaze dancing over the display. "I don't know how."

"Whoever thought we'd wish for palms again," Theodora murmured with a sigh.

"Do we know anyone in Amarillo?" Armand asked. "Any Wraiths who owe us a favor?"

Theodora shook her head. "I'd know if there was." She tightened her lips, looking as troubled as Tag had ever seen her. "It's possible that there's nothing we can do."

"No," Ferris said. "There's one thing we can do. We can identify the real spy and once we know his plan, we might be able to interrupt whatever he has planned for Tupperman."

"Long shot," Tag said. "And against the clock."

She was startled by the fierce look Ferris cast her. "He's my friend. He's innocent. Trying to save him is the least I can do."

She felt chided when he turned back to his work, dismissing her. She stared at him, unable to deny her sense that Ferris wasn't exactly the kind of person she'd assumed he was.

And that made him even more interesting.

"In my people's view of the universe, this world is a realm of shadows," Kara began, aware of how closely Tupperman was listening. "The real world exists parallel to this one and is a place of abundance and joy. The evils that plague us here are unknown in the real world. The two realms exist simultaneously and they overlap. Some people, the ones we call seers, can spot the places where those worlds connect."

"They can see into other realms?" Tupperman asked.

"And more. They can also cross through the portals to the other realm and sometimes return. Most of us make that transition only once, when we die."

Kara glanced at Tupperman and he smiled encouragement. "My mother was fascinated by the Eye of Glass. She was haunted by visions of it. It had been buried shortly after it was created and long before my mother was born. Yet, my mother was drawn to its precise location. Whenever she went missing, they found her there, peering down as if she could look through the barrier of earth to the glass. She told me that it was a portal between this shadow realm and the real one. She said that one of her earliest memories was of the Bright Ones taking her there."

"The Bright Ones?"

Kara nodded. "Like most peoples, we have a story about how the world came to be."

"Tell me," he urged gently.

The story was as familiar to Kara as her own name, she'd heard it so many time. "In the beginning, there was only light and chaos, a swirling disorder that was inhabited by beings of pure energy. We call them the Bright Ones. Their essence fills everything in the universe, or maybe they are the essence of the universe. The world doesn't just exist because of them: it evolves and changes because of the will that they bend upon it. Growth is a mark of their presence. When seeds grow, when children grow, when love grows, it is a sign of their presence. If ever everything halted, it would be a mark of their abandonment."

Tupperman nodded understanding.

"So, they created this shadow world, perhaps as a place where their desire for growth could manifest, perhaps as a mirror of the perfection of the real world. We people were created by them, formed of mud in the darkness of caves and given life by the breath of the wind." She held out her hand. "It is taught that fingerprints are the mark of the wind swirling into our bodies to fill us with breath."

Tupperman smiled.

Kara smiled back. She had always liked the whimsy of that story and she was curiously pleased that he liked it, too. "The wind remains in service to the Bright Ones, taking them messages and carrying all words to their ears. They see all and know all, partly because the wind does its task so well. That is why a person must take care and say only those words that he or she would have the Bright Ones overhear." Tupperman nodded again. "And so it is said that we were created to inhabit this shadow world. The Bright Ones showed us how to live, how to sow, how to harvest and how to respect the world they had created."

"Where are they now?"

"They are everywhere and nowhere, as they always have been. But, although once they were commonly seen in our shadow world, they are less often seen in these times. Only our seers hear them, but mostly they dream of them."

Tupperman stretched out his legs.

Kara watched him, choosing her words with care. "It was said the Bright Ones taught that this shadow world would be destroyed by fire. When that happened, they would return and lead us from this shadow world to the real world. There we would be united with all of those who had crossed between the worlds before us."

"When will that be?"

"It is said that we would know that the destruction of this world was at hand because the ground would wither and the crops would fail. Children would sicken and we would experience both hunger and disease, as we had never before. The Bright Ones said the stars would follow them first to the real world. Then the moon and the sun would follow the stars, leaving the shadow realm to fall into eternal darkness. And so, the ground has withered and the crops have failed. Children have sickened and we have both hunger and disease as we have never had before." She turned to look at Tupperman. "And four years ago, the stars disappeared."

"On September 22" he said, much to her surprise. "I remember. There was a shower of fallen stars, then darkness."

He looked away then, thoughtfulness claiming his features. Kara wondered where he had been on that night and what he had lost.

Maybe she had lost enough for both of them.

Maybe the fact they had both experienced loss was what drew them together.

She knew what came next in her story and hadn't intended to share it. The change in Tupperman's demeanor, though, and her sense that they had much in common, gave her the strength to say it. "My daughter disappeared the night the stars went out."

Tupperman's hand closed over hers and she welcomed his warmth. "What happened?"

She was convinced in that moment that he could be no angel. He was a man, a man with wounds as painful as her own. Kara turned her hand within his and held fast to his fingers, drawing strength from him.

"She was only four years old. I thought she was in bed, asleep. I saw the stars falling, and I went to get her. It was so marvelous. I wanted her to see. She'd been sick and I wanted her to see something that would make her smile. I didn't realize the stars would disappear forever." She paused, cold with the memory. "But she was gone. Completely vanished. Her bed was empty. I looked everywhere, then I went to the Eye of Glass."

Tupperman watched her closely. "Why?"

She took a deep breath, grateful that he had asked her such a question. "Because it is a mirror and a portal. Because there are those who look into it and see more than they should."

"Like what?"

"I don't know. My mother insisted that it should be cleared and it finally was, with considerable effort. My daughter was fascinated by it, so that was the first place I looked when she was missing."

"Just like her grandmother," he said, proof that he listened.

Kara nodded. "I don't know what either of them saw in its darkness, but they couldn't tear themselves away from it once they looked. I was sure she would be there." Her voice faded.

"She wasn't."

Kara shook her head. "Or anywhere else. It was cold that night. Too cold. We looked all night long, and we never found a trace of her."

"And since then?"

Kara shook her head again, her tears welling.

"But that doesn't mean she's dead..."

"It does," Kara said quickly, not wanting to chase false hope again. "She was sick. She was dying of thyroid cancer. Even if she hadn't disappeared, she wouldn't have lived long." Her tears spilled. "I did everything I could for her, but it wasn't enough. I should have taken her away instead of staying in my mother's house."

Kara closed her eyes. She didn't want to remember another one of her failures. She didn't want to relive the pain of Dionta's loss.

She forced herself to remember how her friends and relations had enfolded her in a circle of warmth and love. She thought of how they found her weeping on the Eye of Glass, how they had practically carried her home, how they had stayed with her, how they had insisted she eat, how they had continued the search. And when it all proved to be futile, they had helped her to celebrate her daughter's life and mourn her loss.

They'd had a funeral, even without a body, because Old Sam said it would give Kara's grief a focus. He was right: she could think of that grave, as empty as it was, instead of thinking about vultures devouring her beloved daughter. She could think of Dionta beside her grandmother in the cemetery, under the care of her grandmother in the real world.

Old Sam and the others had been so kind. Kara owed them all so much.

She became aware that Tupperman's hand had tightened over hers, his grip resolute. The contact was more than welcome and Kara clung to his hand.

"You were not a bad mother," he asserted quietly, naming her deepest fear with startling accuracy.

"You can't know that."

"I can. You feel such pain in her loss, and your love for her fills every word. She was everything to you. I can see it. And her loss devastated you."

Kara stared at his strong hand, welcoming his compassion, hoping he was right.

"A bad mother wouldn't be tormenting herself four years later," Tupperman added.

Kara couldn't answer him, but she was grateful for his confidence.

"You haven't told me yet," he continued several moments later. "Why did you go east?"

"A long time ago, my mother said that after the stars went out, the portal should be opened to the Bright Ones. She said the portal should be opened on a total eclipse, on the sixth total eclipse after the disappearance of the stars. We didn't know what it meant, not until the stars did disappear."

He looked at her. "Who can open the portal? Only a seer?"

Kara nodded. "But we have no seer any more. We have no one who knows the ritual or can open that portal." She lifted her gaze to meet his. "So I went to the Oracle, to ask for her help."

"Why?"

Kara shrugged. "The Oracle is the only other genuine seer I know. I thought that if I could talk to her, she might help us." She gritted her teeth in annoyance. "But the Watchful Host ensured that I never spoke to her. Not in three weeks of trying. I'm sure the

Oracle didn't even know I was there." She flicked a look at him, watching his reaction. "They banned me from the building yesterday."

"Why?"

Kara felt her lips tighten. "I became somewhat vocal in my impatience."

"Imagine that," Tupperman said, affection in his tone. "That it took three weeks is impressive." Kara chose not to answer. "Why were you chosen to go?"

"I offered. I should be a seer. It should be my task, but I can't do it. It was my responsibility to try to solve this. I owe my people that much." She heaved a sigh. "I couldn't just wait and watch, Tupperman. I couldn't stand aside while our future was lost. It was a long shot but the only chance we had. I had to try."

His smile was fleeting. "No. You would never stand aside." He seemed admiring of the trait that many others felt a flaw and Kara felt warmer as he watched her.

She was alive.

He was holding her hand.

"And there are men with green eyes in New D.C.," he added quietly.

Kara nodded and averted her gaze, but didn't release his hand. Her pulse raced and her mouth was dry. Tupperman's thumb began to slide over her hand in a smooth caress, a touch that awakened Kara from head to toe. She found herself staring at his hand, at his sure grip of her own, and thinking of how she would like to caress him.

Slowly.

"When will that sixth eclipse occur?"

"Saturday."

She felt his surprise. "Tomorrow?"

Kara nodded. "It makes a kind of sense. The sun and the moon will seem to disappear during the eclipse." She held Tupperman's gaze. "Maybe for only a few moments."

"But maybe forever."

Silence stretched between them, and there was only the warmth of Tupperman's hand for Kara.

"You said that most people cross through the portal only once, when they die." Tupperman's voice was quiet.

Kara knew he had guessed her true motivation then and once more felt a connection with him. She met his gaze, letting him see her anguish. "Yes. They go to the real world, to await us there."

"So, if the portal is not opened and the shadow realm ends..."

"Then I will never see Dionta again."

Tupperman held fast to her hand, his gaze locked with hers. Kara saw respect in his eyes and a compassion that made her want to weep.

And a heat that she could not deny. When he reached for her with his other hand, Kara didn't move away. Tupperman eased away her tears, his touch gentle on her face. "Then we will have to ensure that doesn't happen," he said, as if it were the easiest thing in the world.

Before Kara could argue with him, Tupperman leaned closer and kissed her again.

Kara closed her eyes, opened her mouth, and kissed him back, needing Tupperman's touch.

She didn't need to see his back anymore.

But she wanted to bear his child more than anything in the world.

In the baggage car of the train, a large duffel bag was dragged from the back of the rack. The identification and routing tag fastened to it was removed. A counterfeit baggage tag, identical to the original except for the passenger name and destination, was affixed to the bag instead.

The bag was then tugged into the aisle of the baggage car and dropped heavily. Blood began to seep from the end of the bag.

The perpetrator left the baggage car as silently as a shadow, shoving the removed baggage tag into his pocket.

He stopped in the lavatory to cut the tag into small pieces. Then he flushed the pieces, washed his hands, and returned to his seat.

Meanwhile, blood pooled on the floor of the baggage car, inviting discovery.

V

Delilah frowned as she considered the news her mother had brought. It was troubling that Micheline was so insistent about those three words, especially as they had no obvious connection. The four of them—Montgomery, Lilia, Delilah and her consort, Rafe—were in a small garden courtyard in the official residence of the Oracle. Delilah and Rafe's son, Thomas, was proud to be the center of attention and moved between his mother and grandmother with excitement.

It was chilly in the late afternoon, as if there might be a hard frost that night, but none of them seemed to be in a hurry to move inside. They'd have to go in for dinner and after that, she imagined, Thomas would quickly fall asleep.

She closed her eyes, trying to summon a vision. All she could see were showers of gold dust, which made no sense. She became aware that Rafe was watching her closely and that he understood what she was doing. She tried to empty her mind, to leave space for a prophecy, but no verse filled her thoughts.

Maybe she was pregnant again. The power shifted and changed with the rhythms of her body.

"You can't force it," Rafe said softly as his hand landed on her shoulder.

Delilah smiled at him. "I know. The more I want the vision, the more it tends to be evasive."

"Foresight isn't supposed to be like ordering lunch," Lilia said firmly, her mother's blunt conclusion making everyone smile.

"It's a good thing Lil isn't the one with your gift," Montgomery added. "She'd try so hard to control it that it would just leave her forever."

"Are you suggesting I have issues with control?" Lilia feigned shock while everyone laughed.

There was a chime inside and Delilah recognized the sequence of tones.

"O'Donohue," Rafe said, also recognizing the herald of a visit from the President. He got to his feet and went to escort the other man to them.

"Does he visit often?" Lilia asked.

"I'm not supposed to say," Delilah said mildly.

"Are there really underground connections between the two official residences?" Montgomery asked, but Delilah just smiled.

"Thomas wants to show us something," Rafe called from the doorway. O'Donohue lifted a hand in greeting from the room behind Rafe, his gaze flicking over the faces of Delilah's guests. He gave her an intent look and she nodded once to indicate their trustworthiness. Then the two men leaned over a table with a surface that was a large digital display.

The group in the courtyard rose as one, Lilia picking up young Thomas and balancing him on her hip. "You're getting big," she charged and he giggled.

"What is it?' Montgomery demanded, striding on ahead. His gaze danced over the display.

"A new satellite image," O'Donohue said, touching the screen to magnify the middle of it. "We don't get new scans as frequently as we used to, so there's no definite call on how long it's been like this."

All Delilah could see was a dark shadow, one that was roughly circular, in the middle of the image. "It almost looks like a lake."

The darkness fluttered then. "An eye," Lilia said.

Delilah's sense of malaise redoubled.

"It's glass, a lake of glass in the desert." O'Donohue made the image bigger and they all leaned closer. There were white shapes in the dark lake, almost like birds in the night. O'Donohue pulled up a sequence of images, then linked them into a run of animation.

The wings fluttered, more like moths slamming into a glass

barrier than birds. There was something horrifying about the sight, and Delilah felt sickened by it.

"What's wrong?" Lilia asked, putting her hand on Delilah's arm.

"They're trapped. They're doomed."

"How clearly can you see them?" Lilia asked.

Delilah had to sit down. "They're angels," she whispered. "Can't you see them?"

"They're just white shapes to us," Lilia said.

"Where is this?" Delilah demanded, her voice sharp.

"New Mexico," O'Donohue replied. "The white shapes only appeared briefly, as far as we know, during the last full moon." He tapped and another image appeared, one of the same lake but without any white images in it.

"What could it mean?" Montgomery said, his tone thoughtful.

"We don't know," O'Donohue replied and Delilah heard how difficult it was for him to make that admission.

She felt dizzy then. Rafe put his arm around her and she leaned her forehead on his chest, keeping her eyes closed. "Where in New Mexico?" Rafe asked.

"The old test site." O'Donohue looked around and clearly saw that the others didn't understand. "The original test site for the first nuclear bomb."

"Trinity," Montgomery said.

Delilah caught her breath. "Joachim," she added. "Angels."

Her gaze trailed to the image again. Angels trapped under glass. No wonder she felt ill.

"Tupperman took a train to California last night," Montgomery mused. Rafe opened a data link for him and he pulled up a train schedule. "How much you want to bet he's on the cross-country express that gets to Albuquerque tonight?"

Delilah felt rather than saw the electric look exchanged by the three former angels.

"We have to go there," Rafe said.

"No," Delilah said, raising her hand. "Not us." She gestured to herself and Rafe as she picked up Thomas. She shook her head at O'Donohue, then nodded at her mother and Montgomery. "Only you."

"And Joachim," Montgomery said, taking Micheline's hand.

Delilah nodded and Rafe ceded. It was right this way. She knew it, although she didn't know why.

Tupperman took Kara's hand. "My turn," he murmured, then led her from their seats. There was a shower cubicle at the end of the train car, where all the hygiene facilities were located. He knew from experience that the amount of water would be pitiful, but the cubicle would offer privacy.

The woman across the aisle clicked her tongue in disapproval.

Tupperman didn't care. He was glad he'd had his scars removed. Now he wondered if the impulse had come to him as part of a divine plan. The possibility filled him with a hope he had almost forgotten, a conviction that all would come right in the end.

The weight of Kara's hand in his reinforced that belief. He was awed by her resilience and her strength, that she could stand so tall after all she had endured. She had loved and lost, but that only gave her the strength to love again.

And the conviction that love was worth the price.

Her faith restored his own.

There was no line for the cubicle, given the early hour. Most passengers were still sleeping in their seats. The horizon was just touched with the rosy hue of the dawn, a reminder that Tupperman would reach his destination all too soon and face his challenge. He glanced at Kara, surprised to find her looking uncertain.

It was an expression he'd never expected to see on her features.

She smiled, obviously seeing his surprise. "I'm not sure what I'll do if you have scars," she whispered.

Tupperman smiled at her. "What will you do if I don't?"

Her eyes twinkled and she smiled, her reaction so in tune with his own that Tupperman hastened to open the door. A dim light illuminated the space within. It was lined with stainless steel, the mirror-like surface reflecting the pale light. The cubicle was roughly square, maybe four feet on a side, with a lidded bin that served as a bench on one wall. There was a hinged compartment in the wall above that, as well. A trio of nozzles were fitted in the ceiling. It was clearly intended for one person but they entered it together. Tupperman bolted the door behind them and took advantage of the confined space to steal another sweet kiss. She was like a drug in his veins, one that left him dizzy and delighted, and hungry for more.

"Show me," Kara urged, her eyes alight.

Tupperman opened the bin and folded his jacket into it. Then he caught his shirt at the hem, crossed his arms in front of himself, and pulled it over his head. Kara's gaze danced over his pseudoskin and she watched with wide eyes as he unfastened it at the neck. He peeled the dark heavy garment down, working slowly to ensure that it wasn't damaged, revealing his skin to her in steady increments. She lifted one hand to touch his bare shoulder and Tupperman caught his breath at her caress.

He pushed the pseudoskin down to his waist, pulling his arms out of the sleeves.

"Turn around," she commanded and he did. He heard Kara exhale with pleasure. "It was a lie," she said, as if she'd never doubted it, then her hands slid around his waist. Her lips were on the back of his shoulder and her breath fanned his skin. Tupperman simmered with newfound desire.

"A lie," she repeated, and he turned to catch her in his arms.

Their kiss was hungry this time, utterly without reservation. Tupperman had the sense that she would devour him, that she couldn't get enough of him, that he would be consumed by her desire. She was without restraint and her passion fed his own. Her hands roved over his bare skin, awakening him to a pleasure previously unknown. Her mouth was soft and sweet, her kiss ardent and demanding. She bent to close her mouth around his bare nipple, but Tupperman suffered only the barest touch before he backed her into the wall.

He unfastened the buttons on her jacket and pushed the garment over her shoulders. She laughed when he spun her around and unfastened the back of her dress, then she pushed it past her hips herself. She stepped out of the voluminous skirts, then jammed them into the bin with a disregard that communicated her view of the S&D regulations for women's dress.

The sight of her black corset, laced so tightly around her waist, stole Tupperman's breath away. The contrast of her dark undergarments against the rich gold of her skin was striking and exotic. He unlaced her with impatience and cast the corset aside.

Kara arched her back and stretched with obvious relief.

She was beautiful. He cupped her breasts in his hands and held her captive against the wall as he bent and suckled her. Her nipples tightened and she moaned as he caressed her.

It was only the beginning of the pleasure he was determined to grant her.

He could smell her arousal and his own erection strained against his pseudoskin. She reached for him, but Tupperman spun her around so that she was seated on the lid of the bin. He tugged off her boots and removed her stockings, reveling in the sight of her nudity. He stood back to watch as she unfastened her hair and shook its ebony length over her shoulders. It was straight and thick, like a river of black silk. Her eyes shone with an anticipation that made him hurry.

He shed his own boots and trousers, then eased off the pseudoskin. He had no sooner removed it than Kara's hands were on him, running over his skin, exploring and exciting him. They kissed again, stumbling toward the shower stall in their ardent embrace, touching and tasting and teasing each other.

When Kara closed her grip around his erection, Tupperman caught his breath and broke their kiss.

"You want me," she said with the directness he associated with her. Her eyes sparkled, her vigor for life and its possibilities intoxicating him. "I want you." She arched one brow. "What shall we do about it, Tupperman?"

He dropped to his knees before her, urged her thighs apart and kissed her. Kara dropped to sit on the bench again, as if her knees couldn't support her any longer. Tupperman urged her to lean back and braced his hands on her thighs, opening her to his kiss.

He bent and closed his mouth over her wet heat, kissing her intimately. He cajoled and teased her, wanting only to ensure her pleasure. He felt her skin heat and her pulse accelerate. She moaned and her hips bucked against him in demand. Her reaction thrilled him. Tupperman closed his eyes, flicking his tongue against her as her clitoris grew harder. He felt her nails digging into his shoulders and her feet arching even as he held them in a firm grip. He provoked her with deliberation, wanting to hear her release. Kara began to writhe and to make incoherent noises. Tupperman didn't relent, but drove her higher, tormenting her with pleasure.

When he was sure she couldn't stand any more, he slid his teeth against the turgid peak.

Kara cried out in pleasure, her entire body convulsing and her thighs locking around him as she came. Tupperman didn't let go, but held her fast, even as she shuddered against him. He kept her safe and secure, so that she could savor her release.

He thought she might doze after such a powerful orgasm, but she caught her breath and framed his face in her hands. She smiled at him, those dark eyes dancing. "Maybe you are divine, after all," she teased and he chuckled. "I saw gold," she whispered then. "A shower of gold."

"Golden stars?"

"I don't know, but it was beautiful," she whispered in awe. She rose to her feet and kissed him with an ardor he could not refuse, overwhelming his senses with her and nothing else. When his eyes were closed and he was captive to her kiss, she spun him around and pushed him down to sit where she had been. She straddled him immediately and caught his face in her hands. She smiled into his eyes, then kissed him with new vigor.

Tupperman was lost in the sensation of Kara. His arms were full of her, his tongue danced with hers and he could smell her pleasure. He spread his legs wider, then eased one hand between her thighs, loving how she caught her breath when he touched her slick heat.

"Not again," she whispered into his kiss.

"Why not?" He caressed her and she moaned, welcoming both his kiss and his touch. He fingered her and teased her, liking how she became wetter once again. Her nipples were taut, brushing against his chest at intervals, her hands remained locked around his head. He glanced down to see her toes braced against the floor, her feet arched with a grace that made him even harder. She was wet and ready for him, squirming on his lap in her desire to be satisfied. Tupperman gripped her hips to pull her closer, but Kara broke her kiss and evaded him.

"Not so fast as that," she chided. She was on her feet, tormenting him with the sight of her beauty. She reached for the controls and inserted a credit. Water dribbled out of one shower nozzle. It fell over her in a feeble cascade, more like a shower of diamonds than a true spray. The droplets clung to her hair and slid over her breasts, making her look jeweled.

Tupperman stood up and reached back into the storage bin. He drew out a fistful of credits and put them on the ledge. It was all of the money he carried, but he was ready to spend every cred on this time with Kara. It might well be the last intimacy he shared with a mortal, and he would make it one to remember forever. He piled all the clothing into the storage space, jamming her skirts on top of his pseudoskin, then closed the lid once more to keep their clothing dry.

She reached for him with a smile and he pushed three credits into the receptor. This time, the water gushed over them from all nozzles, soaking them and making Kara's skin slick with water. Tupperman took a handful of the liquid soap and washed her down, working up a lather that shone against the gold of her skin.

He backed her into the wall and laved her breasts, one in each hand, the lather running between his fingers as his thumbs teased her nipples. Kara arched her back, her hair wet against her head, and ran her tongue across her lip.

"Temptation," he murmured.

"Speak for yourself," she replied, then pulled him close for another searing kiss. Tupperman found himself backed into the opposite wall, Kara's hand around his erection, lather running between her fingers as she washed him with a thoroughness that took his breath away. He didn't know what to think when she cast him a playful look, then his credits were being pushed into the slot and the water was rushing over him once more.

When he opened his eyes and shook the water off his face, Kara dropped to her knees and took him into her mouth.

Tupperman was shocked, but the sensation weakened his knees. Her lips were both strong and soft, her movements demanding and arousing. The sight of her buttocks and her feet beyond was so sexy that Tupperman didn't want to blink. He caught her shoulders in his hands, loving the combination of her strength and delicacy. He felt himself get harder and thicker beneath her caress, felt the heat rise within him as his heart pounded with greater intensity. His desire burned but he knew that once wouldn't be enough.

"Have mercy!" he murmured and when she laughed, he shook a finger at her. "Not this way, not the first time."

She smiled with a pleasure that lit her eyes. Then she pushed him back to the floor of the cubicle and straddled him once more. She took him into her wet heat in steady increments, her slow pace making Tupperman groan. Only when she was completely settled on him, and he was buried within her did she smile at him. His knees were bent and he was crammed into the space. He looked up at Kara with the dim light playing around her dark hair and she was almost in silhouette.

"Now you're mine," she said in playful threat. She moved over him, and he heard himself moan at the sensation. She laughed and reached for his credits, shoving a number of them into the receptacle. The water spewed over them both, making her skin slippery and turning the cubicle into a steamy paradise.

She moved over him with deliberation, teasing him as he had teased her, ensuring that his pleasure mounted as high and lasted as long as possible. Tupperman abandoned himself to her, letting her set the pace. He was caught between the conflicting desires to both gain his release and have this moment last forever. He was hard, he was throbbing, his heart was pounding, there was only Kara in his world. He had his hands locked around her waist and could see her breasts swinging over him as she moved with grace and power.

When she suddenly bent over him and kissed him, those breasts were crushed against his chest. The water was pouring over him and he was lost in the spell she cast. He reached impulsively between her thighs, fingered her hot sex, and pinched her hard. Her heat locked around him as she came again and Tupperman surrendered.

He roared as the orgasm ripped through his body, taking him to untold heights and sending fire through his body. He came and came, unable to stop, unwilling to have the moment end, the pulse of Kara's release leaving him shaking and spent.

She kissed his temple, her wet hair trailing across him. "Truly divine," she whispered and he smiled for a heartbeat before she kissed him.

The quality of the security vids was garbage. Ferris gritted his teeth and searched for another, hoping to find just one useful image. The bars were dark, as a rule, and filled with shadows, the public readers relegated to far corners, probably because they didn't generate that much revenue for the establishment. The bar owners tended to focus the camera on the till, so the public readers in the bars weren't always in the field of vision. The last one had been, but there'd been people at the bar, eliminating any chance of seeing who was using the reader behind.

Ferris found the next appropriate vid-feed and pulled it up to the display. The reader was in clear sight for a change.

"They even sprang for illumination," Tag said by his elbow. He supposed he'd get used to her ability to sneak up on him.

"Our luck some huge guy will sit right in the vid-feed at the right time," Ferris muttered.

"I wonder if it's luck or design," Tag replied. Theodora and Armand came to stand behind Ferris to watch.

Ferris glanced up at Tag, thinking she might be on to something, but Armand pointed at the display. A man approached the public reader. The time was exactly right. He was tall and broad-shouldered but wore a hood. He sat down at the reader, carefully keeping his back to the bar itself.

"It's design," Armand said through his teeth and Ferris had to agree. "He's choosing readers that aren't well recorded."

"Do you think that's Pierce?" Theodora asked, but it was impossible to tell.

Just then there was a crash on the vid, like a window breaking. A man swore and Ferris realized it was the bartender. The bartender lunged to the left, probably to the broken window. Maybe they had a display of some kind. But as soon as the bartender moved away, another man, one who had been sitting at the bar, suddenly flung himself at the till. The bartender swore and a fight ensued. The other patrons shouted and backed away, several holding on to their drinks. One screamed.

More importantly the man at the reader glanced over his shoulder.

"There!" Theodora said, but Ferris had already slurped the image of his face and enlarged it. He stared at it incredulous.

"Jackson," he whispered. "It's Jackson."

Had Jackson framed Tupperman? Had he been working alone, or with Pierce?

Where was Jackson now?

Ferris and Tag exchanged a glance, then simultaneously began to search the databanks of the Watchful Host. Tag tossed Ferris a link, and he realized she'd gotten into the shift schedule.

"On leave," Ferris said.

Tag snorted. "Bullshit. He took a helicopter." She flung the image of the requisition across the display. Ferris snagged the identifying number and searched for a flight plan.

"Ten creds it's New Mexico," Tag said.

Ferris snorted in his turn, feeling a sudden camaraderie with her. "I'd have to be an idiot to take that bet."

To his surprise, Tag laughed. He looked up to find her eyes sparkling and her features transformed. She was remarkably pretty and his mouth went dry as she smiled at him.

Their gazes clung for a moment, then she inhaled sharply and turned away. Ferris found his heart thundering as he waited for the flight plan. He'd never felt like this, not even with Delilah, and he had to wonder if a new adventure was beginning.

If so, he couldn't wait to discover where it led.

Kara was delighted. Her interval with Tupperman was perfect, exactly how lovemaking between a man and woman should be.

She didn't want it to end.

Kara and Tupperman washed each other, spending the last of Tupperman's credits, and dried each other in silence. They dressed in the confined space—a feat not without its challenges—smiling at each other. Kara felt like a lovesick fool, but she wanted the feeling to last. It had been years since she had felt so light and so optimistic. Even the ache in her lower body had eased, and she dared to believe that she and Tupperman had succeeded in completing one of her goals.

Their return from the cubicle together clearly outraged the matron seated on the other side of the aisle. Kara couldn't help but smile at the woman's expression. As they took their seats, she caught Tupperman giving her a smile.

"You should smile more often."

"I should have something to smile about more often," he countered and captured her hand in his. He looked as contented as

Kara felt.

Then he frowned and looked at her. "That note. What was it written on?"

"A piece of paper torn out of a book."

Tupperman put out his hand.

He clearly had an idea and Kara was curious enough to dig out the paper and surrender it to him. The paper was thin, thin and fragile. It almost was transparent, and certainly the words printed on one side showed through to the other. The edges were a bit ragged and it was dirty, evidence that it had passed through many hands.

"It's from the Bible," Tupperman said.

Kara wouldn't have known. She'd never seen a Bible and didn't know its text very well. It was the product of a different culture from her own. She shrugged, but Tupperman ran a fingertip across a verse that had been underlined. *"The lamp of the body is the eye,"* he read. *"If therefore your eye is sound, your whole body will be full of light. But if your eye is evil, your whole body will be full of darkness. If therefore the light that is in you is darkness, how great is the darkness!"*

The concept made sense to Kara.

"Mark 6:22-23," he murmured.

"What does that mean?"

"It's the location of the verse. You see? This page is torn from the Book of Mark." He showed her the notations and Kara nodded with new understanding.

"Does that matter?"

"I don't know. But we might learn more of who left you this message from the paper itself."

"There are other messages, erased ones."

Tupperman nodded, his eyes narrowing as he studied the remnants of writing around the perimeter of the page. After a moment, he held the sheet against the window and spread it flat with his hands. "This one is a list of numbers," he said.

Kara surveyed the list and shook her head as she indicated the last two. "11:13? 11:21? What do they mean?"

"They might be references to other verses, either in the Book of Mark or others."

"Or they could be something else," Kara felt compelled to note.

Tupperman peered over his shoulder, scanning the car. The other passengers were awakening. "I wonder if anyone has a Bible."

They looked as one at the disapproving woman across the aisle. Kara squeezed Tupperman's hand, then leaned across the aisle to ask for assistance.

"It's never too late for a sinner to repent," the woman huffed, then handed Kara a small well-thumbed book. Kara looked at the volume with awe. It was only the second book she had ever seen and the first she had ever held.

The woman was clearly pleased by this reaction. She straightened her skirts. "You should read the Beatitudes," she instructed.

"I cannot read," Kara lied and handed the book to Tupperman. He leaned back so that the woman would not be able to see his face and Kara turned toward him, as if she were a rapt student. He opened the book and began to look up the verses.

And Kara found herself dozing once again, but this time, her dreams were serene.

The citations made no sense to Tupperman. There was no coherence between any of the verses, as if they were random. He supposed it could have been a kind of code.

Or the numbers might mean something else.

Or they might be irrelevant.

Even if his sense was otherwise. Tupperman stared out the window as the countryside flew past and drummed his fingers on the armrest. It was late afternoon and the sun was fading already. They had left Oklahoma City behind and shared a meal in the dining car. Now the plains stretched flat and empty to the horizon. Kara was sleeping beside him, her head having fallen onto his shoulder, and Tupperman was at ease.

His mood made no sense. He still had to face Lucifer and undertake his challenge. He still had to risk everything to save the lost angels, who were only condemned because he had persuaded them to shed their wings. He still doubted he would survive the ordeal, and he still believed that it would be worth any price to see justice served. He glanced down at Kara's hand and took it in his own. She didn't awaken, but her fingers curled around his in a way that made him smile.

The difference was he now felt he had truly lived. With Kara, Tupperman had experienced a passion beyond anything else, and he already felt a powerful affection for her warming his heart. He understood finally why mortals took such risks for love, because he knew that even now he would surrender a great deal for Kara. If he were so lucky as to triumph over Lucifer, he would return to Kara, fall more deeply in love with her, and love her for all his days and nights. He'd have no need for heaven and its charms, not when he could be with Kara.

That would be heaven on earth.

He understood now why some of the others—Montgomery, Rafe and Armand—had chosen to remain in the earthly realm, even after their missions were complete and they could regain their wings.

Tupperman stared out the window, savoring this curious mix of serenity and excitement. When he thought about it, the abandoned warehouse where he had met angels immediately after they had sacrificed their wings had been a kind of a portal, a way station between heaven and earth.

Did the angels have anything to do with her Bright Ones? There certainly were similarities between the stories, but Kara adored the Bright Ones and abhorred the angels. What was he missing?

He frowned at the whirling sands beyond the window.

"Oh, do bring her along," murmured a familiar voice in his ear. Tupperman jumped and looked around, knowing he wouldn't likely catch a glimpse of Lucifer.

He was right.

"You're thinking you'll surrender anything to defeat me," Lucifer continued. "Why not her? I like a passionate woman, or two."

His laughter chilled Tupperman's blood and even after the sound of it had faded, Tupperman wanted to shudder.

He had to protect Kara.

He didn't believe for one instant that he'd be able to convince her to stay behind when he went to meet Lucifer, and he didn't imagine that he'd evade her in New Mexico.

Which meant he would have to leave Kara while he had the chance. The notion caught at his heart, as deceiving her was a lousy reward after the pleasure they'd shared. But he wanted her to survive, and that was the only way to ensure as much. Lucifer would challenge him in every way, and the price of failure was high. He couldn't fight and defend her, too.

He'd kept his promise to her, but their ways had to part.

He should leave her immediately.

Even if he didn't want to go.

Maybe, just maybe, he'd survive the challenge with Lucifer and manage to return to her.

Maybe, just maybe, Kara would have him if he did.

She was everything mortals were supposed to be. She was passionate and forthright, a woman who followed her impulse and her desire. She was clever and principled—when she made mistakes, she tried to set things to rights. She was strong and thought quickly. She did everything with vigor, living full out every moment of her life.

If nothing else, she had shown him the possibilities and made him finally understand the appeal of this realm.

If just in time to leave it.

He hoped with unexpected urgency that she had conceived his child.

There was another reason to ensure her safety.

His decision made, Tupperman picked up his bag. He took one last long look at the woman who had so completely seduced him, then got to his feet. He carefully stepped past her, returning the Bible to the woman across the aisle as he considered the train's layout.

Ahead of them were the shower facilities at the front of this car, then the first class car and the engines. To the rear of the train were at least two more passenger cars—he hadn't gone past the one with the reservations computer—then the dining and baggage cars.

"The dining car is back there," the woman said, her mood helpful since Tupperman had borrowed her Bible. She'd mistaken the reason for his hesitation, but Tupperman thanked her and strode in that direction. He had to think it would be easier to slip off the back of the train than to saunter through the first class cabin.

Then he had to find a way to get to the Eye of Glass, alone.

VI

In Kara's dreams, a dark shadow loomed behind Tupperman, a menace that would snatch him away. She awakened with a jolt, her breath coming quickly. She reached out a hand, only to discover that Tupperman was gone.

So was his bag.

She was instantly awake and on her feet.

"He went to eat," said the lady across the aisle, pointing toward the dining car.

With his luggage? Kara thought not.

He'd *left*.

She didn't doubt that he'd made a selfless and noble choice, probably believing that she'd be safer without him. But leaving her wouldn't be quite that easy.

"Thank you." Kara smiled at the matron, seized her own bag and headed in pursuit.

To her astonishment, she almost collided with Tupperman in the dining car. He was marching toward her, his features pale.

"What is it?"

"Just turn around, now," he said through his teeth. Kara glanced over his shoulder and saw two conductors come out of the baggage car. They looked dismayed as they conferred quickly. One reached for the train intercom.

"Passenger Tupperman, please identify yourself to a crew member. Passenger Tupperman, identify yourself, please."

"What's going on?" Kara whispered, even as Tupperman ushered her back toward their seats. "They'll find you there."

"I'm not going there," he muttered.

"What's wrong?"

When they reached the small junction between two passenger cars, Tupperman pulled his laze. He put its muzzle against the lock on the door to the car they'd just left, and melted the lock. Then he urged her into the nook that was out of sight of both cars. There was a dull echo of further announcements being made and Kara's heart began to pound.

She wouldn't let them take him away.

All she could see was the intensity of Tupperman's gaze; all she could feel was the grip of his gloved hand over hers. His voice dropped low. "There's a duffle bag with a corpse in it, bleeding in the baggage car."

Kara caught her breath.

"The bag must have my name on it." He swallowed, his gaze flicking past her to the unsecured door. "I was going to pass through the car..."

"And leave the train." Her tone was hard. "You were going to leave me."

Tupperman ignored that charge, but his eyes flashed. "I saw it and stopped to look. I was there when the conductors came."

"So, they found you beside the body." Kara tightened her grip on his hand. "Did you touch it? Can they link you to it?"

He shook his head. "They won't get any prints, but I saw the man inside."

The way he swallowed told her all she needed to know. "You know him," she guessed.

"I did. I know he died because of me."

"You didn't kill him."

"Not directly." Kara shook her head in confusion, but Tupperman urged her back toward their seats. "Go." His eyes blazed. "You don't know me and you never did."

"But what about you?"

"I'll do whatever I have to do."

She'd thought he was grim before, but he was doubly so in this moment. The announcement echoed again. Kara held fast to his hand. "No, I'll go with you...."

"No!" Tupperman had time to protest before the handle turned on the door that led to the forward car.

Their gazes met in alarm.

Tupperman pulled his laze and mouthed the word 'Go.'

Kara wasn't going anywhere without him. If Tupperman didn't believe her, she'd show him.

Actions spoke louder than words anyway.

Kara took the single step to the door, hiding Tupperman's presence with her body. She smiled at the conductor through the window in the door. She turned the handle, taking her time, and slid the door open, managing to block the passageway with the fullness of her skirts.

"I thought all of the members of the Watchful Host were angels who shed their wings four years ago, the night the Oracle summoned them," Tag said.

"Sure," Ferris said, wondering why she wanted to review something so obvious. This time, he spoke with a measure of impatience. "It's a corps of fallen angels, all of whom shed their wings at the same time."

She enlarged Jackson's image on Ferris' display. "Interesting then that he's been here more than four years." She pulled up images of Jackson, time-stamped for years before that night. "He's changed names a few times. Jenkins. Jacques. Jackson."

"Did Tupperman know?" Armand asked.

Ferris shook his head, shocked. "I don't think so. I think he would have commented."

"But Tupperman helped the fallen angels when they arrived, didn't he?" Theodora asked. "How could he *not* know?"

Ferris was going to agree, but then he thought of something. "What if Jackson shed his wings before Tupperman?" He knew Rachel had shed her wings before Tupperman, but wasn't sure when the angels had started to volunteer.

"That only opens all of human history in terms of possible time frames," Tag said. "Fortunately we only have decent vid for fifty or sixty years." She headed back to her display and frowned at the screen. Ferris wished he could give her some hint where to start.

"There's an incoming vid from Montgomery," Armand said suddenly and they all turned to watch.

The vid was from a satellite and showed a dark circle on the ground. As they watched, fluttering white shapes appeared within it. Ferris was reminded of moths flying around a light, throwing themselves at it in their urge to get closer. Although the sequence didn't last long, there was something deeply troubling about it.

"Birds," Theodora said.

"Moths," Ferris guessed.

"An illusion?" Tag suggested.

Armand showed the sequence three times. "He said it's in New Mexico, that the white shapes are new. This only appeared briefly during the last full moon."

"Where exactly?" Theodora asked.

Armand gave the coordinates and Tag caught her breath. "I heard the site had been cleared again."

"Where?" Armand asked.

"The Trinity test site," Tag explained. "Where the desert sand was fused into green glass."

"Green glass?" Ferris echoed, and when she nodded, he rose to his feet in his agitation. "That's got to be where Tupperman is going. He had a piece of green stone."

"When did he get it? Maybe that will give us a lead," Theodora said.

Ferris shrugged. "He's had it for a few years. But he was toying with it more, especially that last night."

Armand sat down hard. "Has he had it for four years?" he asked.

"Why would that matter?" Theodora asked.

"We each undertake a mission. I know he declined the restoration of his wings that night four years ago." Armand looked at Ferris. "He might have accepted another mission, when he chose to stay."

Silence fell in the room then, those shapes fluttering as the vid ran again.

"It was as if earth had been touched with the fire of the angels," Tag whispered, seemingly apropos of nothing, and Ferris turned to look at her.

"What do you mean?"

She slanted a glance at him. "That's what a witness said about the Trinity test. What if it wasn't an analogy? What if the angels helped?"

Ferris frowned. "But angels must have foresight. They would have anticipated how nuclear bombs would be used." His fingers rose to his throat, his scar feeling unusually tight. It was the angelic host who had healed him. "Surely angels wouldn't have done such a thing?"

"Don't you know? Wouldn't you remember this?" Theodora demanded of Armand.

He shook his head. "That's part of the transition. When the wings are cut away, many powers and much knowledge disappears. Most of what I knew was forgotten, except for those details I was believed to need in this realm."

"For your mission," Tag said and Armand nodded.

"Maybe it was just one angel," he continued. "Jeqon is Jackson's angelic name," he continued. "He's said to be the one who led the fallen angels into temptation. What if he led men into temptation, too?"

Tag nodded. "What if he shared what wasn't his to give?"

"But why?" Theodora asked.

"Because people do," Tag said darkly.

"But angels don't," Ferris argued.

Armand looked grim. "Unless he was serving another master," he said tightly. "One who tries to tempt us all."

"I wish you could remember the greater plan," Theodora said. "There must have been one."

"I knew my quest was important," Armand said. "I volunteered because it was right." They all turned as one to the vid again as his tone turned thoughtful. "Trying to repair the mistake of one of our own would be as right as right could be."

"Could those be angels?" Theodora asked softly, her voice unusually hesitant. They fell silent, both because none of them knew the answer and none of them wanted to think about that possibility.

If they were angels trapped in the glass, Ferris knew that Tupperman must be planning to help them.

But how?

"Good evening," Kara said to the agitated conductor, knowing that Tupperman was hidden from view behind her.

"Excuse me, madam," he said, almost bouncing in his anxiety to pass her. "There's an emergency on the train."

"Oh, my! Is it safe?"

The conductor made an impatient sound, then pushed past her. Kara stepped into the car and slid the door shut behind her back. She heard a laze sighting and closed her eyes, then leaned dramatically backward to block the window in the door.

"Are you all right?" a passenger asked from beside her and she smiled weakly at him.

"Just a little motion sickness," she said, touching her stomach. "I'll be fine."

The man smiled in turn and settled back. "My kids can't stand these trains for the same reason."

Kara was saved from continuing the conversation by the audible firing of a laze. The conductor shouted, there was a scuffle, then the door was hauled open behind her. Tupperman's heat was at her back. He slammed the door behind himself and fired his laze at the lock, melting it so the door would have to be forcibly opened.

The outraged conductor began to pound on the door, demanding release.

Kara exhaled in relief that Tupperman hadn't killed him.

"Go," he instructed.

"Not without you," Kara insisted and when he glared at her, she went. They were complicit now, which was exactly how she wanted it to be.

The passengers in the car leapt to their feet and the train began to slow down.

Kara thought she saw a familiar face as she hurried through the car in front of Tupperman—Derek's ghost, again?—but with the pace Tupperman set, she had no chance to look back.

The next car was the one with their seats. Tupperman flung open the door and Kara practically ran the length of the car, sounds of pursuit echoing behind them. The announcements continued to drone. The woman who had been seated across the aisle from them gasped in horror as they passed.

"Not you?" she cried, but neither Kara nor Tupperman answered her.

They were passing the washroom facilities when the train began to slow. Outside the windows, Kara could see flashing lights of police vehicles racing alongside the train. Amarillo couldn't be that close, as the plains ran flat and empty.

Multiple trucks. Kara stared in amazement. She knew there was more canola readily available here, but there were at least four police trucks. "They want you badly," she said to Tupperman. "They've planned this, to intercept the train outside the city and leave you no escape."

"And someone with a lot of resources is paying the bill."

"Sounds like you know who."

He smiled and didn't reply.

Behind them a conductor blew a whistle. "Tupperman!" he shouted. "We only want to talk to you!"

"Bullshit," Kara muttered.

"Exactly," Tupperman agreed.

The door to the first class car was locked. Tupperman shot off the lock and kicked it open, only to reveal a number of well-dressed passengers startled by the interruption.

"There are only the engines after that," Kara said.

And more security. The first class conductor was pulling a laze.

The conductor behind them shot at them, and they ducked in unison. "We're trapped!" Kara said.

"Not yet." Tupperman fired at the lock and hinges of the platform door of the first class car. It fell off, revealing a slice of prairie lit by flashing lights.

"You coming or staying?" Tupperman asked.

Kara smiled. "I'm with you."

"I had a feeling," he muttered, but didn't look very disappointed. "Hang on, then."

She locked her arms around Tupperman's neck as he fired a shot down the length of the car. A woman screamed. A conductor shouted. The police sirens wailed and an alarm emanated from the train itself.

Tupperman jammed his laze into its holster and caught Kara around the waist. The wind ripped the pins out of her hair as he swung out the door and around the end of the car. There was a ladder there, and he pushed her up it to the top of the train.

Kara looked but there were no tunnels ahead, just windswept plains, police cars and a city far in the distance. The sky was enormous and open, as sure a sign as she was close to home as possible. She was glad to have her sturdy boots when they ran down the length of the train, as they helped her to keep her footing on the flat top of the cars. If the train hadn't been slowing, they never would have managed it.

They got to the baggage car, then swung in unison over the end. Gorse grew thickly on either side of the tracks, although Kara didn't think it would break their fall much.

"Roll when you hit," Tupperman instructed. Kara didn't even have time to nod before he caught her close and leapt from the moving train.

Shots fired all around them, the laze fire illuminating the sky. Kara swore. She'd hit the ground before she realized Tupperman had sheltered her with his body. She did the best somersault she could manage in her skirts and came to a halt with Tupperman sprawled on top of her.

There were sticks in her hair and in her teeth, but the shadow of the plants surrounded them. Tupperman rolled and she followed him, moving away from the tracks under the cover of the scrubby plants.

The train emitted a hoot and began to accelerate again. Kara saw a conductor at the open back door, the light silhouetting his figure, before the door was closed again.

That conductor had been a fool to stand like that, even for a moment. If Tupperman had wanted to kill him, it would have been easily done.

But Tupperman hadn't really injured anyone. As they moved away, the train picked up speed, racing toward Amarillo. The police cars fanned out, searching the land for some sign of her and Tupperman. Kara's heart was pounding, but she felt safe.

Her bag had contained nothing of importance. Her hat and veil, clothes she never wanted to wear anymore. She didn't need Tupperman's map to get him to the Eye of Glass. She didn't know why he was going there, but she trusted that his objectives were noble.

And if he wanted her help, she'd give it.

Kara had recognized immediately that he hadn't known anything about that bag and its contents. He'd been more shocked by the news than her, even if he did feel responsible for that unfortunate man's demise.

She had many questions for Tupperman, but for the moment, they had to survive.

Tupperman suddenly threw himself over Kara, flattening her against the earth. His move drove the breath out of her, but she knew he must have done it for a reason. He was still and heavy, the combined weight of his pseudoskin and his body keeping her crushed against the ground. Kara closed her eyes and leaned her cheek against the ground for a moment, glad to feel the earth again.

Tupperman's gloved fingertip landed on her lips, but Kara didn't need the warning. She'd felt the tension in his body. She looked around and saw the lights of police vehicle coming directly for them, closing fast.

They'd been spotted.

Kara felt Tupperman draw his laze. He put his hand over her head, but Kara peered through his fingers, not wanting to miss anything. The police Jeep came closer, and closer, and she was sure they'd be found because of the pounding of her heart.

A laze shot lit the night and singed the earth just inches away from them.

Kara gasped.

Tupperman fired twice in rapid succession, shooting out the headlights on the Jeep. The driver braked hard, sending the vehicle into a spin and launching a volley of dirt. Tupperman was on his feet, Kara right with him, amazed that he could run so quickly with the pseudoskin.

"You run quietly enough to be one of us," she whispered. He smiled, then looked left and right, peering into the shadows.

The Jeep engine revved behind them, the police in hot pursuit.

"We'll never outrun them," she said, huffing a little.

"You know how to drive?"

Kara glanced at him, certain her surprise in the question showed. "Sure. Don't you?"

Tupperman didn't answer. "Even without headlights?"

"Easy. We did it all the time to save juice."

He was clearly pleased, even though they were running hard. "We need an obstacle," he muttered. "Something that will compel them to get out. Ideas welcome."

So they could steal the Jeep. Kara nodded, liking how methodically he thought, and that he thought of them as a team. "There's a river." At his quick glance, she smiled. "I can smell the water."

Tupperman nodded, glancing back at their pursuers who were driving slowly. She thought he would ask her for directions, but he surprised her again. "You lead."

Warmth rushed through Kara that he trusted her so much to follow her in the dark. She changed their course, glad the river was close. The ground underfoot quickly became rocky, which slowed the Jeep even more. The distance between them and their pursuers increased slightly. In the distance, Kara could see the other vehicles now turning toward them to assist.

She knew the river was nearby, but the ground fell away so fast that she halted almost on her toes.

"Perfect." Tupperman scanned the gully, then they leapt over the side as one. At his gesture, Kara backed against the lip of the ledge. They both flattened themselves so they wouldn't be visible from above. Tupperman bent and picked up a handful of fist-sized stones, then indicated that she should be still.

Kara could do that.

She was impressed that he could do it, too. Most people had little talent for stillness. Tupperman was a rare exception.

The Jeep halted, gears grinding as it was parked. Kara guessed that it was twenty, maybe thirty feet away.

The engine remained running.

Kara barely dared to breathe as the policemen decided what to do. Tupperman's eyes gleamed as he listened, then he arched a brow.

Kara hadn't heard anything, but the Jeep doors slammed. She heard heavy footsteps approaching. Two men. In boots. Probably with their lazes pulled. She cast Tupperman a triumphant smile, but he began to pitch stones into the shallows. The first one landed with a splash that made one policeman exclaim.

Tupperman threw each stone incrementally farther than the last. The stones landed in the river and reeds, splashing in succession.

Like departing footsteps.

"I can't see them," complained one policeman. From the sound of his voice, he was right above the hidden pair.

"The infra-red isn't picking them up either."

"But they're running to the north. I heard them."

"Must be reeds interfering with the signal. Piece of shit."

"Let's go while we can still hear them."

The pair leapt over Kara and Tupperman and landed in the dirt just ahead of them. One swore and straightened more slowly, as if he'd turned his ankle. The other was already marching down to the water.

Tupperman had put one hand on Kara's stomach, his fingers splayed to indicate she should wait. She'd thought he might jump the policemen, or fight them, but he remained as still as a statue. Instead of pulling his laze, he silently picked up another two stones.

The policemen hurried down to the river, then the second one stumbled in the mud of the shallows. He swore again, and his partner said something scathing to him. They strode on together, the second one falling further behind. As Kara watched, Tupperman aimed one stone, then flung it hard.

It hit the second policeman in the back of his helmet with enough force to make him stumble. He was immediately knee-deep in the mud and clearly unable to regain his balance easily. He swore a third time as he wobbled, then fell into the river with a splash.

The more vigorous one pivoted and fired at them. Tupperman shoved Kara behind him, even as he flung another stone. Kara heard a crack and the policeman shouted.

He stumbled backward and there was a splash as his laze fell into the river.

This time, he swore.

"Same lousy visors," Tupperman muttered as if unsurprised and disappointed.

Kara stared at his back as she realized the truth. He *was* a cop.

"Go," he urged in a whisper, his laze braced in both hands as he covered her back.

Kara didn't hesitate. She was over the lip of the gully, running toward the Jeep in record time. Even before she was inside, she knew it was a fine piece of equipment. The dashboard was lit, the indicator showing that the fuel tank was full. She got in, shut the door and flung open the passenger door.

She heard the exchange of laze fire, but was busy turning the Jeep around. A shot cleared the roof of the Jeep and she ducked just as a man hurled himself into the passenger seat.

"Go!" Tupperman cried, but Kara had already pushed the accelerator to the floor.

The two of them hunkered down low as the Jeep raced across the open plain. The skies were obscured the full moon and its light, at least. Kara drove around rocks and potholes, her experience in driving Derek's truck in the dark serving her in good stead. She drove right across the train tracks and headed south to circumnavigate Amarillo.

"Who taught you to drive?"

"My husband. When we were dating. I had to drive home at night, off-road, no lights, and not get a scratch on the truck."

"Or?"

Kara shook her head. "Not then. He never hit me until I was pregnant."

Tupperman inhaled sharply. "Bastard," he muttered with disapproval.

She felt him studying her as she wound them through a cluster of shrubbery. "You could kick me out, turn yourself in, say I abducted you."

Kara loved that he was offering her a choice, and one that would probably work. She shook her head. "Not a chance, Tupperman. You're stuck with me."

"Sounds like a good deal to me."

"That's only because you haven't realized that you'll have to tell me what you're really doing here."

He was spared from answering, for the moment at least.

There was a click, then the dispatcher's voice echoed through the Jeep. "Vehicle 7659. Vehicle 7659, come in, please. Identify yourself, please, 7659."

Kara pointed to that same number, stenciled on the dashboard. Tupperman looked at his laze, winked at her, then fried the receiving unit to silence.

"It'll still have a tracking device," she said.

He was already nodding. "Get us to as remote a location as possible and I'll take it out."

"You know where it is."

"No, I know what it looks like, but that should be enough."

"Because you're a cop, too." She spoke without doubt and knew that she'd surprised him.

He sighed. "A smart partner, too. I'll have to be more careful if I mean to keep any secrets from you."

"Or you could just tell me all of the truth."

"You'd never believe it."

Kara glanced at Tupperman, surprised by his comment, and it was just enough time. She didn't see the truck on her left, also driving without lights.

"Look out!" Tupperman shouted and lifted his laze.

He fired, and Kara swerved, but the other vehicle plowed into the left side of the Jeep. The Jeep skidded sideways, and she was sure it would roll.

That was the other driver's intention, anyway. He or she meant to kill them.

Kara wasn't quite ready to die just yet.

Against every expectation, she'd discovered since boarding the train in New D.C. that she had a lot to live for.

All Points Bulletin
Imperative Update for All Law Enforcement and Military Officials

For Amarillo and Surrounding Area

2105-11-20
1730

A suspect in the murder of a Watchful Host soldier has evaded arrest and fled the scene in a stolen police vehicle. The fugitive is Caucasian with a shaved head, approximately six foot two and 190 pounds. He is armed with at least one laze and is a quick shot. It is believed that he has served recently as a police officer. There is a woman in his company, who may be his hostage. He is considered to be armed and dangerous, but Captain Jackson of the Watchful Host requests that he be taken alive for questioning.

Links: <u>Map of Area</u>
            <u>Vid from RailRepublic</u>

Tupperman couldn't believe it.

Kara looked as if she were enjoying herself. She was a good driver—no, she was an excellent driver, completely in tune with the vehicle, even though he doubted she'd ever driven a police Jeep before. She seemed to intuitively understand its capabilities and limitations.

He'd suspected her skills before they were broadsided, but that incident made the truth clear. He'd been afraid the collision would make the Jeep roll and explode, but he hadn't counted on Kara.

The other car hit them hard, making the tires skid as the Jeep moved sideways. A cloud of dust surrounded the vehicle and Tupperman coughed as it came through the filters. Kara hit the brakes, sending them into a spin. She turned the wheel so that they spun harder. As soon as the other vehicle lost contact, she accelerated and steered out of the skid as if she drove like that all the time.

Tupperman took a shaky breath and released his grip on the upholstery.

"It's not over yet," Kara murmured, watching in the rearview mirror. "Brace yourself."

Tupperman barely had time to respond before she hit the brakes hard, nearly stopping the Jeep on its front fender. Tupperman was sure the back tires came off the ground. She turned the wheel hard and the Jeep lunged to the right, even as the other vehicle swept past them on the left. Tupperman saw the other vehicle send up a swirl of dust as that driver braked. She pushed the accelerator right to the floor, and Tupperman tried to hide his terror as they raced across the plains.

He couldn't see a thing, just darkness ahead. Night had fallen with remarkable speed, helped by the cloud cover and their distance from the city. He could hear rocks hitting the underside of the vehicle and gorse being crushed beneath the tires.

Kara leaned forward, her expression avid. "Come on," she whispered. "Come get us."

The other driver did exactly that. The vehicle roared up behind them and bumped them hard from behind. The Jeep lurched forward, but this time, Kara didn't accelerate.

"Let him think he's winning," she said softly, just before they got bumped again.

She steered wildly then, as if losing control of the vehicle. She lifted her foot off the accelerator so the Jeep slowed and the engine of the vehicle behind them roared. Kara steered to the right as the yawning darkness of the river bed appeared on their left.

"Relax," she said without looking at Tupperman. "I knew it was there."

"Of course," he managed to say.

The other driver roared up on the right side, and Tupperman saw that it was a police truck. The driver veered suddenly, then smashed his truck into Tupperman's side of the Jeep. The Jeep leapt to the left, closer to the river bed, and the door protecting Tupperman from harm rumpled with disconcerting ease.

They were driving on the lip of a precipice, as far as he could see, although Kara seemed to be completely at ease. It appeared to be a long drop to Tupperman and one that wouldn't end well for them or the truck.

"I'm assuming you have a plan," he said. Meanwhile, he watched with horror as the truck veered toward them again. He closed his eyes and gritted his teeth as it crashed into his door. He feared the Jeep would slide off the edge of the river bank.

Then Kara braked harder than she had so far. Tupperman bit his tongue and braced his hand against the dashboard.

They came to a full and sudden stop.

He looked up as the other truck disappeared over the lip of the riverbank. There was a loud crash, a bang, and then an explosion. The flames lit the night with orange fury and Tupperman saw the bend in the river that curled right in front of them. If she hadn't stopped so hard, they would have plunged into the river gorge as well.

"You knew," he accused as Kara grinned.

"I remembered. Didn't you look at the line of the river?"

"I was busy trying to steal this Jeep."

She nodded. "My mother used to say that you should pay attention. If you focus on one thing to the exclusion of everything else, you might miss something that you'll need to know later."

Tupperman leaned his head back and closed his eyes, the speed with which the tension abandoned his body leaving him exhausted. "I think I would have liked your mother."

"I know she would have liked you." Kara put the Jeep in

reverse, turned it and drove toward Amarillo. "We'll pass town on the south side, then you can remove that tracking device."

"I'll guess that you know the way to the Eye of Glass from here."

She smiled without looking his way. "You'd be guessing right. If we're lucky the clouds will hold for a while."

"Why?"

"It's almost a full moon, Tupperman. We don't need the illumination." She settled into her seat, adjusting it as she drove and tweaking the position of the mirrors. "Now, tell me a story."

"What?"

"You heard me. And you know what story I want to hear. Take your time, Tupperman, but tell me all of it."

Tupperman considered his options. He didn't have very many, particularly since Kara had helped him to escape. That she had done so was telling of her character, her passion and her vitality.

He wanted to make love to her again, one last time

But first, he owed her the truth.

Or at least, the part of it that wouldn't alienate her completely.

VII

"You were right," Tupperman said finally, just when Kara thought he wouldn't confide in her. "I am a cop."

"In the east?"

"New Gotham." He paused. "Special Operations."

Kara nodded. She could believe that he'd be good at collecting secrets and passing unobserved. That explained his pseudoskin, his laze, and possibly his trip west. "I assume you have a specialty."

He nodded and looked out the window at the night. His confession was low. "I gather intelligence for the Watchful Host."

Kara was so startled that the Jeep swerved a bit. "You're in alliance with the fallen angels?" she demanded. "You're kidding me."

Tupperman shook his head.

He is one of them...

Kara remembered the note left for her and understood its message better. Tupperman was associated with the Watchful Host, that made him one of their company if not of their kind.

She had to get past her own prejudices in order to help Tupperman survive. If he was allied with the fallen angels, she believed he had good reason to do so. "What's that got to do with the Eye of Glass?"

"Nothing." He heaved a sigh and rubbed his own chin. Kara had the sense that he was editing the story, but then, he was probably sworn to keep some secrets for the state.

She wondered if she could convince him to share even those.

She wondered if it was wicked of her to want to do that.

She decided to let him tell her what he would.

"You've probably noticed that the Watchful Host have been unlucky in recent months," he said finally, giving the word "unlucky" a particular emphasis.

As if he didn't believe that luck had anything to do with it.

Kara kept her tone even. "Lots of them killed in the line of duty."

"Eighteen." He bit off the word, as if he took it personally. "I gave the Watchful Host the intelligence that led to their being ambushed," he said softly. "I am responsible for those deaths."

"But you didn't kill them."

"Not with my own laze, but with my own mistakes."

The air was charged between them for a long moment. "I don't think you should blame yourself," Kara said. "These things happen..."

"They don't happen to me," Tupperman interrupted tersely. "And if they happen to me, I try to make things right."

"Why the Eye of Glass?"

"Officially, I'm on leave. Unofficially, I have an appointment there."

"Someone wants to meet you."

He nodded and fell silent.

Kara thought of the note that had been addressed to her, the luggage in Tupperman's name, and had to ask. "Who knew you were going?"

"No one."

"Except the person who made you the offer."

"This isn't his handwork."

"How do you know?" Kara was outraged. "You're being set up, and the only way to defend yourself is to figure out who's behind it all. It makes sense that the person who made the offer put all this in place..."

"No, it doesn't." He gave her a steady look. "It was an offer from the Devil himself."

"Lucifer?"

"Lucifer."

Kara thought of the shadow she'd seen in her dream and

shivered. Tupperman continued to talk. "If you believe in angels, you have to believe in devils. If you believe in fallen angels, you already believe in Lucifer. If you believe in good, you have to understand that evil completes the circle. Lucifer offered to give me a chance to save the souls of those lost angels."

"In exchange for what?"

"Possibly my own soul."

Kara stopped the Jeep abruptly, horror filling her. "No. You can't do this. This isn't your responsibility..."

"It is my responsibility, Kara. There's no evading it. I have an obligation to make things right." He reached out and touched her cheek with a fingertip when she would have protested. "I have to do this." Tupperman was resolute. "If I survive, I will find you. Because if I do survive, it will be because of you."

Kara closed her eyes, trying to blink back her sudden tears. It wasn't possible that she should lose him so quickly. It wasn't right that he should undertake such a heroic task and not survive it.

But she didn't think that Lucifer would play fair.

She felt his lips brush hers and leaned across the cab, welcoming his touch. His kiss was hungry and hot, and filled her with new yearning. She had to have him again—and again and again—before she lost him. She had to fill her memory with the look and the feel of him—because if there was any chance she'd only have memories, Kara wanted them to be as rich and plentiful as possible.

Tupperman pulled away, his eyes shining as he smiled at her. "Temptation personified," he murmured and Kara smiled.

"Get rid of that tracking device, Tupperman, and I'll show you some temptation."

She only caught the flash of his grin before he was out of the Jeep and cool air flowed into the cab in his absence. She bit her lip and considered what he had told her. She knew she couldn't change his mind.

She also didn't believe it could really be his fault that so many of the commandos had died. Had someone betrayed him? Kara knew there were many who wanted the Watchful Host disbanded or eliminated, and was herself no fan of angels.

The note. She pulled it out of the pocket in her skirts and flattened it on the dash just as Tupperman got into the passenger seat again. "I put it under your front tire," he said. "It'll be crushed when you drive over it."

"And then?"

"And then they'll go to its last recorded location, which probably isn't far from here. They'll conduct a search radiating outward from that point."

Kara didn't have to hear more. She hit the gas and the Jeep charged into the night, making a satisfying crunch as it began to move. She shoved the piece of paper at Tupperman. "What if they're dates? The second to last one is 11:13. Wasn't that the date of the last failed raid?"

She felt the quickening of Tupperman's attention, then he crumbled the paper into his fist. "Except there are five numbers," he said. "And if they're dates, the last one is tomorrow."

"But you're one of them," she said. "Why don't you have scars on your back?"

"I had them removed," he admitted. He reached out and claimed her hand. "I didn't want to deceive you, Kara, but I couldn't resist you either."

She didn't answer, just drove onward, astonished that one man could challenge her convictions so thoroughly in such a short time.

Not a man—a fallen angel. Maybe that made the difference.

He'd lost her.

Tupperman saw as much in Kara's eyes when she guessed the truth of his nature. He didn't want to have lies between them, but he still didn't want to lose her. The cab of the Jeep fell into silence after that, leaving each to their own thoughts as they headed steadily west.

Tupperman would have given everything he possessed to know what Kara was thinking.

At least she hadn't kicked him out of the vehicle.

The engine started to sputter just after dawn.

"We're running out of juice," Kara said unnecessarily. "There won't be anywhere to fuel up around here."

"We couldn't, even if there was," Tupperman replied. "There will be an All Points Bulletin on me by now. It's only a matter of hours until they find the truck."

"Probably the darkness slowed down the search, then."

"Probably." Tupperman scanned the plains ahead of them. It was all so desolate and barren. Kara had followed the river most of the night to keep her westward course, but it was the sole indentation in the landscape. He saw only empty land stretching in every direction. No mark of humanity. And swirling dust. The land was arid, the vegetation sparse. Having lived all of his earthly existence in cities—and before that, perpetually hearing the thoughts of other angels—the solitude struck awe and fear into Tupperman.

It meant that it didn't really matter where they stopped.

Kara pumped the accelerator as the engine sputtered more loudly. "What are you looking for?"

"A good place to burn the Jeep." He was glad that the details gave them something to talk about.

She looked at him in surprise. "It's not a bad vehicle."

"It's full of evidence. They might not yet know the identity of the woman forced to travel with me, but they'll figure it out if they can inspect the vehicle."

"Fingerprints," Kara said.

"Hair, skin flakes, you name it. And for all I know, there's a hidden recording device in here." Tupperman shook his head. "No. It has to be destroyed."

"Any choices?" she asked. "I can get maybe another hundred yards."

"Any place is as good as the next. I've never been anywhere so empty."

She smiled unexpectedly. "Isn't it wonderful? Nothing but earth and sky."

Tupperman looked at her in surprise, but Kara was clearly serious. "It's desolate."

"It's perfect," she countered, to his amazement.

The Jeep's engine sputtered, choked and died. The vehicle continued to roll a little more on the flat ground, then came to a halt. Tupperman was out of it in a heartbeat, rummaging through the kits packed into the back of the vehicle.

There were flares and a flint, which would work well enough for him. He grabbed a first aid kit, and filled a pair of canteens from a water reservoir. There were some energy bars, which would be better than nothing to eat.

Kara came to his side and rummaged in the kits, taking a few things herself and jamming them into a bag before he could identify them. She would know better than him what would be useful in this terrain. He was glad to have her as a fellow traveler and told himself it was foolish to wish for more.

He took the flint and the flares, wedging one flare into the console between the front seats. There was a small can of kerosene for a lamp, and he emptied it all over the driver's seat. He left that door open, then backed away with Kara.

"Ready to run?" Tupperman asked Kara and she nodded. He lit the second flare, and when it was on the verge of shooting sparks, he aimed it at the soaked seat.

The upholstery ignited immediately and began to burn. Tupperman held the flare steady and it shot five more sparks into the interior of the vehicle. Kara covered her face as black smoke began to rise in rolling waves from the burning Jeep. The flames crackled and jumped, burning ever more hungrily, until the entire interior was in flames.

Tupperman tossed the flare into the vehicle and they turned to run.

They were hundreds of yards away when the vehicle exploded with a resounding boom. Kara jumped then looked back. "That's what I call destroying a vehicle," she said with satisfaction. "There will be nothing left of it."

"That's the point."

She held up a hand for silence, her gaze skyward.

Tupperman heard the helicopter a full minute later than Kara had heard it. She pointed to a shadow cast by a cliff far ahead, the only shadow within sight, and he nodded. They didn't speak, just raced onward together.

Tupperman knew there wouldn't be any shadows to hide them in a couple of hours.

Kara couldn't dismiss her sense that they were being followed. But not by any representative of the Republic's authority.

The hair was prickling on the back of her neck, as if someone was watching her. Driving, she'd felt repeatedly that they were being stalked by a phantom vehicle. She thought she caught glimpses of it, thought she heard the hum of its engine. But each time she stopped or checked the mirrors, there was nothing there.

Was she just paranoid?

Or was their stalker skilled?

She eyed a plume of dust in the distance, unable to shake her sense that it had been roused by a vehicle. The dust swirled onward, progressing far ahead of them. She supposed another person could be headed in a similar direction, but was discomfited even after the dust faded from view.

With every passing hour, she was more worried about Tupperman. She could see that he wasn't used to the heat of the sun, much less to walking in this blowing sand. He wouldn't remove his pseudoskin, even though the weight of it made it doubly difficult for him to continue. She was impressed by his strength, but concerned as well.

Everyone had limits, even fallen angels. Tupperman had ceded to her expertise in other matters. He ate and drank as she instructed him, acknowledging that she knew the terrain and its demands better than he did.

She'd have to try again to convince him.

"If only you'd take off the pseudoskin," she said as he fell behind her. "You don't have to toss it away; just take it off."

"What's the difference? I'll still carry it."

"It's making you work harder, by ensuring that you can't sweat. You're going to boil alive inside that thing."

Tupperman wiped the perspiration from his brow and gave her a wry look. "I seem to be sweating well enough."

"Take it off."

"But it provides some protection against laze shots."

Kara spread her hands. "I don't have a laze."

"Whoever is tracking us does," he said grimly and she realized he shared her suspicions.

Still she asked. "How do you know anyone is tracking us?"

"I'm accused of murdering a member of the Watchful Host. I've evaded capture and stolen a police vehicle. I've destroyed that vehicle and may have a hostage." He gave her a hard look.

"They're tracking us. Trust me."

Kara nodded, reluctant to tell him of her observations.

"And if they shoot to kill, I might just survive long enough to ensure that you escape." He trudged beside her with determination. "The pseudoskin stays."

Kara was surprised that he was enduring this for her. "I can take care of myself."

"I got you into this." Tupperman removed his gloves, his expression grim. "I'll get you out."

Kara didn't want him to suffer so much for her, but she knew a losing argument when she heard one. In a way, it thrilled her that he would bother. No man had ever put her needs first. She bit her lip, feeling that she should tell him about her own sense that they were being followed, but knowing it would only make him more determined to keep on the pseudoskin.

"We need to find shelter," she insisted, knowing she had to ensure he didn't exert himself too much.

He nodded agreement and wiped his brow again. "Which seems an unlikely prospect, given that we've stepped off the edge of the world."

"We've stepped back *into* the world, you mean."

"You're actually glad to be here?" His incredulity made Kara smile.

"It's my home. We're within the four mountains that define the legacy of my people." She pointed them out to him in turn, naming them with affection. "When we are home, all is returned to harmony."

"I'll remember that when they shoot at us."

Kara laughed.

He smiled crookedly at her. "How can this be home? It's a wasteland."

"Look more closely," Kara instructed. "The land is alive, and there's enough to sustain those who aren't greedy in their demands." She gestured to a cactus and named it in her own language. "This plant's presence tells me that there is water below the sand, not that deep, or the plant would die. There is water within the plant, as well, and its flesh can be eaten."

Tupperman's expression remained skeptical. "With those thorns, it doesn't look inclined to share." They climbed a rise then, his breath coming more heavily with the exertion. "I thought deserts were flat."

"This wasn't desert until recently. It was arid, but not this dry."

He spared her a glance. "Let me guess—the change is the angels' fault."

"Why do you say that?"

"Because everything is the angels' fault to you."

She turned away from the consideration in his eyes, knowing the concession he wanted from her. She wanted to give it to him, too, but didn't want to surrender too much too soon.

She'd made that mistake before. "You're right. And it was the angels' fault. The creation of the Eye of Glass changed everything, even the climate. The winds blow differently now, and the sun burns hotter."

Tupperman didn't reply, just climbed to the rise and looked over the vista ahead. "Not a soul," he murmured, as if that were a bad thing.

"Perfect," Kara agreed, ignoring his surprise. "There!" she said, pointing to an old house far ahead. She guessed that it was made of wood, since it was faded to silver by the sun. It would be deserted and would offer them shade. Tupperman turned his steps in that direction and seemed to get a second wind. He drained his canteen and tossed back a salt tablet as they descended the gentle slope. They matched steps again, and Kara shivered with sudden gooseflesh.

Tupperman looked at her.

"Someone walked across my grave," she said with a shrug.

"Is that what your mother would have said?"

Kara nodded and he smiled. He took her hand as they approached the dilapidated building. It was no more than a shack and the wind pushed through the gaps between the wooden planks, making a lonely whistle. Kara saw the water pump in front of it and dared to hope. It was possible there was still water that could be pumped out.

Tupperman needed to rehydrate. She dropped her bag beside the rusty pump and grasped the handle. It squeaked and complained from disuse.

Tupperman peered inside the tumbledown shack, kicking at the sand as he explored it. "Nothing but dust," he said. "There's nothing but dust and sand." He propped his hands on his hips and squinted at the roof. "I suppose it'll be better than nothing, though. And you love it here?" He shook his head when Kara smiled. He tossed down his own bag and began to kick sand out of the shack with his feet.

Just as Kara heard the gurgle of water rising in the pump, she heard another sound that made her freeze.

It was the rattle of a snake's tail.

Tupperman must have disturbed one sleeping in the shadows in the shack.

She spun to warn him, but something cold landed against her temple. It was the muzzle of a laze and the feel of it brought her to an abrupt halt. Tupperman had frozen in place, his gaze fixed upon her.

"What a good wife you are, Kara," Derek said into her ear. "Bringing my intended victim right to me."

At the sound of his voice, everything made perfect sense. Kara hadn't seen Derek's ghost: she'd seen Derek.

He wasn't stalking her: he was stalking Tupperman. He'd written the note to her and included the list of dates. He'd always hated angels. He had to be part of the team assaulting the Watchful Host.

And they were planning to let Tupperman be blamed for their deeds.

She loathed Derek with new force then and resented that he planned to steal something more from her.

In that instant, a new fear came to her. Had Derek stolen Dionta away? Was that why the child had disappeared so completely? He was her father. She'd never considered the possibility because she'd believed him dead.

Derek set the sight on the laze, the weapon still pressed against Kara's temple. The audible click made Kara stop breathing.

The rattler continued to shake its tail. Kara could see it now, a large Western Diamondback, coiled in the back corner of the shack. It had to be six feet long, and it was annoyed. A city-dweller like Tupperman would never have seen it until he'd disturbed it.

"Throw your laze to me," Derek instructed. "Any tricks, and Kara dies."

Tupperman slowly removed his laze from the holster and tossed it into the sunlight between himself and Derek. At Derek's gesture, he raised his hands and stood still.

The rattler shook its tail.

"You are a wily one, Tupperman," Derek continued. "Betraying the Watchful Host from inside the organization, setting their commandos up for ambush."

"You know it wasn't me."

"But I'm the only one who knows it."

"I doubt that," Tupperman said quietly.

"Don't try to bluff me, Tupperman. You don't have any allies. Not anymore."

Kara caught her breath and Derek gave her a shake.

"There's not a soul in the Republic who will be sad to learn that the fugitive Tupperman didn't survive his flight from the law."

"Even if it's a lie," Kara said.

"Who will prove otherwise?" Derek taunted. "Truth is whatever we insist it is."

"What is the truth?" Tupperman asked. "Indulge me with that. Are you a member of the Brotherhood of Honest Laborers?"

Derek laughed. "I *am* the Brotherhood of Honest Laborers. I run it all. You could think of me as the ultimate avenging angel. You all deserve to die, but I'm the one who's making sure of it."

"Not alone," Tupperman said, his gaze bright.

"Not alone," Derek agreed. "But that story isn't mine to tell."

"A story?" Tupperman asked. "Or is it a prophecy?"

"Don't talk to me about prophecies," Derek snarled. "I might as well have been dead, for all she cared about me. What color are the brat's eyes, anyway?"

Kara caught her breath. He'd referred to their daughter in the present tense.

Was he playing with her?

Or did he not know that Dionta had disappeared?

He shook her head. "Answer me, bitch, or I'll have to teach you about respect again."

"Brown," Kara said. "Just as I told you they would be."

Derek snorted. "Figures you two would find each other," he said. "The spy who is so worthless that he gets framed for betrayal, and the mother who is so uncaring that she leaves her child behind to take a vacation in the big city."

Derek didn't know about Dionta, which meant he didn't steal her or know where she was.

"It wasn't a vacation," Kara said.

Derek laughed. "No, it was a failed quest. Why do you think the Watchful Host really kept you from the Oracle?"

Kara felt a chill slide down her spine.

Derek nodded. "Yes. I told them to. I called in a little favor."

"But why?"

"I told you years ago, you deserve to die. Having the chance to ensure your failure was an unexpected bonus."

Tupperman's eyes blazed. "Go ahead and shoot me," he said. "Do what you came to do. Just let Kara go. She has nothing to do with this."

"My wife's fate is not your concern, Tupperman, but you are mine. The good news is I'm not going to kill you. The bad news is that you won't survive this day anyway."

Kara could feel how much Derek was enjoying the situation.

He continued in a conversational tone. "That snake is a Western Diamond Rattlesnake. Its presence here is just too easy, as if divine will were real."

"No," Kara whispered. No one deserved to die from a snake bite. "No!"

She struggled out of Derek's grip and he backhanded her. She fell to her knees but snatched for Tupperman's laze.

Derek's shot came so close it singed her fingers. She pulled back her hand instinctively and he grabbed her by the hair. He hauled her up in front of himself and pressed the hot muzzle of the laze against her temple.

It burned, but Kara didn't dare cry out.

Tupperman looked livid. Had anyone ever been angry when Derek abused her? His expression confirmed everything she already believed about his nature and made her more determined to fight for him.

"Go kick the snake," Derek instructed Tupperman. "And then reach out to it with one hand."

"No," Kara whispered, but Derek pushed the laze muzzle harder against her head.

"Go."

Kara watched in horror as Tupperman took a slow step toward

the snake. He was going to let himself be bitten, to ensure that Derek didn't kill her. She couldn't believe any man would commit such a selfless act—but then, she had been married to Derek.

Kara knew that Derek would still kill her, even after Tupperman was dead. He'd hit her enough times that she knew he had no qualms about violence. He wouldn't leave a witness alive to tell of this crime.

But he'd take Tupperman from her first and make her watch.

Then he'd possess her again, poisoning her body with his touch.

She hated him with a vigor she hadn't known possible.

"You ambushed the Watchful Host," Tupperman said. "You put that bag on the train, with Rumford's corpse inside and my name on it."

Derek nodded. "And I made sure they found it. Now, the story ends, happily for everyone except you, Tupperman. The clever cop from the big city will have miscalculated. He'll be found dead by the authorities, with no sign that I was ever here. Don't worry. I'll be sure that your pack contains plenty of evidence that you were a secret member of the Brotherhood of Honest Laborers. No one likes a rogue angel."

But Kara did. "I love you, Tupperman."

Tupperman's gaze brightened an increment. He winked at her, as if to encourage her, and her throat tightened.

"How touching," Derek snarled. "Go kick the snake, Tupperman."

Tupperman glanced at the snake, then back at Derek, without moving.

"Do it now or she dies," Derek said.

He set the sight on the laze again.

Tupperman visibly took a deep breath. He looked Kara in the eye. "I love you, Kara," he said, his voice low and hot. Then he strode across the derelict floor and kicked the snake. It rattled furiously and reared up. Tupperman reached out to it with one hand.

And it struck immediately.

Derek chuckled.

Tupperman caught his breath as the rattlesnake sank its fangs into the back of his hand. He grabbed it behind the head, ripped it free and flung it hard into the desert. The snake disappeared in a flash, sidewinding its way across the sand. Tupperman's hand was already swelling, the two fang marks oozing blood.

"Happy?" he said to Derek. "Now let her go."

"Not quite yet. Tell your friend about Western Diamond Rattlesnakes, Kara." Derek encouraged her with a nudge of his laze.

Kara knew this was her chance to give Tupperman the information he needed. "They're poisonous, but they don't always release venom when they bite."

"What's the treatment, Kara?" Derek prodded.

"A tourniquet can help. Sucking the wound doesn't help." Blood was running more quickly from the wounds. Tupperman looked faint and she knew he'd already been dehydrated. "You have to have anti-venom within five minutes to survive. It has to be given intravenously."

"Too bad you don't have any," Derek mused. "Or any chance of getting to a hospital. Where is the closest hospital? Albuquerque? If you could even walk that far." He laughed and shoved Kara to her knees, keeping the laze trained on her. He pushed something into Tupperman's pack that had the emblem of the Brotherhood emblazoned upon it, then picked up Tupperman's laze. "Tell him the symptoms of hemotoxic venom, Kara."

"Numbness, swelling, rapid pulse, metallic taste, confusion, vomiting, delirium."

"Death," Derek concluded with satisfaction.

Tupperman was already trembling. He fell to his knees and Kara saw him gritting his teeth. "Let her go," he insisted. "Let me see that you've let her go."

"I'll release her," Derek said, backing away. "But not until she's far enough away that she can't help you. Thirty minutes should be enough of her for me. I guess you won't be conscious to see how it all ends. You'll have to trust me." He tossed Tupperman's laze in front of the other man, who didn't seem to be able to understand what it was. "Say goodnight, Tupperman."

"No!" Kara cried. She fought Derek, seized her pack and acted as if she was swinging it at him. She made sure she missed and that the bag was flung out of her hands, landing close to Tupperman. She reached after it, but Derek tightened his grip on her hair, and dragged her after him.

"You don't need anything in there now," he snarled. "I guess I'll have to teach you all over again how to obey a man." Kara cowered, knowing that was the only thing that could mitigate Derek's anger. As she ducked her head, she caught Tupperman's quick sidelong glance.

He looked angry and focused.

Was it possible that he was faking his symptoms?

Kara prayed that he was.

She also prayed that he looked inside her pack. She'd taken a snake bite kit from the police car.

By the time Derek looked back, Tupperman was swaying on his knees. He reached for the laze, but fell face-first in the sand. He gasped, shuddered, and didn't get up again.

Derek laughed and shoved Kara ahead of him. "There's a truck beyond that rise. Move it."

Tupperman didn't dare to wait until Derek and Kara were completely out of sight. He could feel a strange dizziness and knew he didn't have long.

Kara had been trying to help him. There was something in her pack.

He ripped open her bag and rummaged through it.

A snake bite kit. It would never have occurred to him to take such a thing, and in fact, it hadn't. He ripped it open, breathing heavily at the sight of the syringe and small bottle.

She'd told him what to do, and he was running out of time.

Tupperman couldn't focus his vision enough to tell if the vial of anti-venom had expired or not. His hands were shaking in truth as he filled the syringe and he didn't have time to strip off his pseudoskin. He rolled it up at the wrist, effectively creating a tourniquet, and had no time to be squeamish. He slid the needle into the exposed vein on the inside of his wrist.

It hurt, but he emptied the syringe slowly.

He considered his symptoms as he did and knew the snake must have released its venom. He could feel his thoughts clouding, as if a fog descended over his mind. He had enough strength to retrieve his laze and lock his hand around its grip, then he collapsed in the sand again. He rolled into the shade offered by the cabin and hoped he'd acted in time. He felt the numbness steal through his body, the venom racing ahead of the antidote.

He couldn't save himself and he wouldn't kill himself.

His survival was up to a higher authority.

Tupperman closed his eyes. He had time to regret his failure, to be glad to have met Kara and request forgiveness for his shortfalls.

All too soon, his world faded to black.

"Gone to ground," Armand muttered. "Just as we thought."

Ever since they'd seen the A.P.B., the reports had become more troubling by the moment. Everyone in Theodora's datahub had been working on intercepting official communication about Tupperman, and it had been bewildering to keep up.

It was worse when the networks descended into silence.

Pierce and Jackson had disappeared into the desert—if they were in communication with the Watchful Host, Ferris couldn't find the datatrail. Tupperman was gone as surely as if he'd never been.

Ferris sat back and shoved his hands through his hair. "We have to tell Delilah," he said to Armand, who started.

"The Oracle?" he echoed. "What do you think she and Rafe can do?"

"They might know something. She might have had a vision." And even if she hadn't, she had the ear of the president. If anyone could intervene for Tupperman, it had to be O'Donohue.

Tag came to lean her hip on Ferris' display. "You can't seriously know the Oracle."

"I grew up with her," Ferris said, his tone dismissive.

Tag's eyes widened. "You're *that* Ferris? The one who saved her from the Daughters?"

"What do you know about it?"

She smiled again. "Rumor and innuendo. Not nearly enough." Her gaze turned assessing. "And here I thought you'd led a charmed life."

"I have. I knew Delilah when she was Twenty-three. I knew Rafe before he was Consort. And I've seen the angels myself."

Ferris ignored Tag's astonishment and turned back to Armand, who appeared to be amused. "We can build a case in Tupperman's defense, presenting the evidence we've gathered about Jackson, and send it to her. She might be able to help him."

"She might be the only one who can," Armand agreed. "Let's do it."

Kara wasn't going to leave Tupperman behind.

He loved her. She loved him. They both deserved a better ending than this.

But she knew Derek well enough to understand that he wouldn't release her alive.

At least not by choice.

She pretended to be weak and contrite, as well as devastated. She begged for Derek's forgiveness, letting him drag her to the truck he'd concealed beyond the rise. All the way, she schemed her revenge.

When they got to the truck, she pretended to be too weak to climb into it.

"Get up, you lazy bitch," he said and struck her across the face. Kara fell back into the sand and remained motionless, as if unconscious.

Derek swore and came after her. "I should leave you here, faithless cow, leave you here to die under the sun." He bent over her, then squeezed her breast in one hand. His voice darkened. "But I've missed you in one way. You'll serve me one more time before I'm done with you for good."

He shoved his laze back into his holster, then bent down to pick her up. He was still an imposing man, but his muscles weren't as strong as they had been. He faltered a little when he lifted her and muttered about her getting fat.

Kara hung on his shoulder like a dead weight, letting him carry her toward the truck. He opened the passenger door and flung her into the seat. He took a moment to wipe his forehead and catch his breath.

Which was one moment too long. Kara kicked him in the genitals as hard as she could. He howled in pain but Kara went for his face. She jabbed her thumb into one eye, twisting his nose with her other hand and he stumbled backward.

Kara seized his laze from the holster. When he caught his balance and looked up at her, she had it trained upon him.

She sighted it as he watched, knowing he'd hear the tone.

He held up his hands and turned on the charm. "Kara, baby, you wouldn't..."

Kara shot him in the crotch.

He shouted and fell to his knees, the smell of singed denim and burning flesh mingling in Kara's nostrils. "You ungrateful bitch," he said and leapt for her. Kara shot him in the face, frying one eye to oblivion.

She cooked his right hand and left him moaning on the desert sands.

"You were going to leave a good man to die in the sand," she said. "I think it's better to leave a bad one to that fate."

Derek groaned.

Kara got into his truck, started it and checked the fuel. It had more than enough juice to get them home.

If Tupperman was still alive.

She kicked up a spray of sand that half-buried Derek and headed back to the shack.

Tupperman dreamed.

He swam in a sea of deepest darkness, a sea that was cold and impenetrable. The cold made his limbs heavy and he felt dragged down, down toward chilly depths. There was a glimmer of light above him, as faint as starlight through the clouds, and he struggled to swim upward to the light. It seemed his lungs would burst for lack of air, that his legs were made of lead, that the water turned viscous and thick.

He surged toward the light with a burst of power, and his head collided with an invisible barrier.

Glass across the surface. Cold smooth glass, offering no grip to his fingertips. He slid his hands across it in desperation, seeking a crack or a fissure or some way to break through it to the light and air beyond.

Just before his body surrendered to the cold, he realized he wasn't alone. He was surrounded by others who similarly crowded against the underside of the glass, trying to escape.

Their skin was tinged blue from the cold. The wounds in their bodies were dripping red blood. Their expressions were that of hollow horror.

And their wings, their luminous white wings were losing their radiance, becoming tinged with black.

At Lucifer's triumphant laugh, Tupperman jolted awake.

Tupperman shook to his marrow. He tasted the perspiration on his own skin and took a deep jerking breath, just because he could. He felt fingertips brush his brow and heard Kara's voice. The tension slid out of him and he slipped into dreams again.

But this time, he dreamed of a blinding shower of gold.

And even without understanding what it meant, he was glad.

VIII

Tupperman was alive.

He was unconscious, just barely in the shade of the shack, his laze in one hand. The snake bite kit was scattered on the sand before him, the syringe used and the vial of anti-venom empty.

Kara had to love a practical man. She bent and listened to his pulse, relieved that it was slower than she'd anticipated. She got the first aid kit and washed the area around the snake bite, then rolled him over and nudged him to wakefulness.

"I can't lift you into the truck, Tupperman," she informed him but he only murmured incoherently at the sound of her voice. He took a deep breath, struggling against something, then collapsed again.

Kara lifted the laze out of his hand and put it in the holster for him, thinking that might reassure him. He didn't move. "We need to get out of here, and you need to help."

It didn't look as if Tupperman would be helping.

Kara left him and drove the truck as close as possible to the shack. She went around and opened the passenger door, then considered him again. He weighed a ton in that pseudoskin.

There was no point in trying to lift more weight than necessary.

If nothing else, he wasn't awake to argue with her. Decision made, Kara tugged off his boots and threw them in back of the truck. She then worked him out of his pseudoskin. It was beautifully fitted, obviously a custom suit, and she was careful to keep from damaging it.

Kara checked the horizon repeatedly for Derek as she worked, but there was no sign of him. He wouldn't be able to move fast, if at all, with those wounds. Kara managed to shove and haul Tupperman into the truck. It was tough enough with him wearing just a T-shirt and underwear, but she managed.

He sprawled in the passenger seat, limp but breathing. It was better than the alternative so Kara took hope where she could find it. Tupperman was the kind of man she'd always hoped to find—even if he was an angel. She hadn't lied when she'd said she loved him. It wasn't just his green eyes and the opportunity to fulfill the prophecy. It wasn't just his good looks or his secretive smile. It was his stillness and his thoughtfulness, his determination to do what was right, his blend of strength and tenderness. His sense of honor.

And now, he might die. Kara tucked a blanket over him with care and checked his pulse again. Was it her imagination that it was returning to a normal pace?

She hoped she was pregnant already. Having Tupperman's child wouldn't be as wonderful as being with Tupperman, but it would be some consolation if she lost him. She'd be able to see him in his child, and she knew it wouldn't just be in the child's eyes. It would make sense that Tupperman's child would have the conviction to save the world.

The child would take after his or her father.

If she'd conceived. Kara wanted another chance, a lifetime of chances.

She put Tupperman's clothes and pseudoskin in the storage area behind the seats, checked the horizon, then got in. She set Derek's laze on the console where she could easily reach it and drove away from the shack. The truck had a compass in the dashboard, but she knew from the four mountains where she was and how to get home.

Dark shadows fell across the sand and Kara jumped, certain that a creature with large leathery wings was close to her. She looked up, frowned as the shadow seemed to vaporize, then tipped her head to look up at the sky.

Vultures were circling overhead. She reasoned that she'd heard their wings, even though she knew they were too far away for that. Their presence told her everything she needed to know about

Derek's chances of survival.

If she wasn't a widow now, she'd be one by the time the sun went down.

That state of affairs couldn't come a moment too soon.

Kara wasn't really surprised to find a whiff of smoke rising from the chimney of her small house. In fact, the sight filled her with relief.

She'd planned to return on this day, at the latest, and she guessed that the others were sitting vigil. They'd want to hear what she'd learned and what she'd achieved. Just a day earlier, she'd dreaded this encounter, but so much had changed. There was hope, but also peril.

She spared yet another glance at Tupperman. His body was still struggling against the venom and he was unconscious. She hated that she couldn't check his vitals continuously while she drove, although she knew she'd done what she could.

Kara stopped the truck right outside the door of the adobe building, then checked Tupperman's pulse again. It had become even more regular. The anti-venom was winning and she said a silent prayer of gratitude.

By the time she reached for the handle on her door, Old Sam was there, opening it for her. The tall and trim man had always had silver hair in her memory, and had the best understanding of the land of any of her people.

"I saw the dust plume," he said simply.

"And you saw it long before anyone else," Kara said. "I'll bet the wind told you about it before it was even visible."

A twinkle lit in his dark eyes. "I have to have some skills, otherwise none of you would have any use for an old man."

"Nonsense!" Kara got out of the truck and dared to give him a hug. She felt his surprise, for touching was not common among them, then he tightened his arms briefly around her. He had been worried. "You have more knowledge and secrets than anyone I know."

Old Sam peered past her into the cab, his brows rising. He said nothing, even though Kara was sure he'd guessed that Tupperman wasn't wearing much beneath the blanket she'd tucked around him.

"He was bitten by a rattlesnake," she explained, feeling her color rise.

"Anti-venom?"

Kara nodded. "He administered it himself."

Old Sam's brows rose even higher and he looked at Tupperman with new consideration. Kara was tempted to tell him what she knew of Tupperman, but the secret wasn't hers to tell.

Bonita and Sousche stepped out of the shadowed doorway. They, too, had moved so quietly that Kara hadn't noticed them.

She'd been away from home too long.

She did feel their searching glances, though. "I never saw the Oracle," she admitted, guessing what they wanted to know. "The Watchful Host kept me away from her."

"Did she get your message, at least?" Sousche asked, the older woman's eyes filled with concern.

Kara shrugged. "I don't know. I don't think so." She gestured to Tupperman. "But I found a man with green eyes. Maybe I can fulfill the prophecy."

Sousche smiled. "Your mother would have been pleased."

But Bonita shook her head. The younger woman was practical to the point of being skeptical about prophecies. "You haven't been gone long enough that we could have a seer by the eclipse," she noted. "Who is he?"

"A policeman," Old Sam said softly and Kara saw that he was fingering Tupperman's pseudoskin. "And yet you brought him here." He didn't question or challenge her outright, but Kara felt his concern.

"I told you. He was bitten by a snake..."

Old Sam took a steadying breath as if he would argue, but Sousche stepped between him and Kara. "Kara's compassion is the gift of her mother," she chided softly. "It is in her to heal."

"It's in a *seer* to heal," Bonita corrected flatly. It was fear that made her tone sharp, but Kara was still stung. "Is this his truck?"

"No," Kara admitted, forcing herself to think of practical details. She decided not to tell them just yet about Derek. "We're probably being followed."

"You are," Old Sam said. He held up two fingers. "By two sets of vehicles." He surveyed the sky with suspicion and Kara remembered the helicopter that had swept over them in the morning. Old Sam's powers of observation were so strong, that along with his knowledge of the natural world, he sometimes seemed to be a seer himself.

Together, they lifted Tupperman from the truck. "He's suspected of murdering one of the Watchful Host," Kara said and the news startled her companions.

Old Sam's eyes brightened. "I like him better." He lifted Tupperman to his own shoulder with ease and carried him inside the house that had once been Kara's mother's home and was now her own. Sousche followed closely behind, Bonita trailing behind Kara.

"The others will come at sunset," Sousche said, revealing that she and Old Sam had discussed it. "Then we'll have to decide what to do."

"Right now, we have to get rid of this truck," Bonita said. "Old Sam, will you come? I could use your help getting back here for the eclipse."

"Ah yes," the older man said, scanning the horizon. "I have an idea how we could lead them astray." He patted Kara's shoulder. "Do not fear, Kara. There must be a purpose in all of this."

"And if there isn't?" Bonita asked.

Old Sam smiled. "Then the world will end anyway. Maybe the Bright Ones will still come to us."

Bonita heaved a sigh, then eyed Kara. "It's not your fault. I know that. I just wish it would all end differently."

"Don't give up," Kara said as she leaned over Tupperman. "I'm not."

"Your mother always said that hope was the most potent force of all," Sousche reminded them and Kara nodded.

She was sure it was true.

And if Tupperman awakened, they could prove it.

Pierce didn't like it. Even though he understood the reasoning behind Jackson dismissing the regional police on what he called the business of the Watchful Host, Pierce had a bad feeling about it. He knew that Jackson was in charge of the investigation to find the leak, but he didn't like how quickly the investigation into Tupperman's destroyed unit had been concluded.

It was almost as if Jackson hadn't wanted anyone to look more closely.

The only explanation Pierce could have for that was the excellence of their forensics team. The haste made him doubt the reliability of the spilled blood as evidence. He wished he'd seen it himself, because he had a hard time believing that Tupperman had captured and murdered anyone.

Particularly one of the angels he'd convinced to shed their wings to aid humanity. It didn't make sense.

But Jackson seemed almost eager to believe it. Maybe he liked finally having a solution to the mystery of the leaked information.

Pierce hoped that was all of it, but something about the situation wasn't right. It had been impossible to ask questions in the high speed helicopter, a choice of transit that revealed the Watchful Host's resolve in seeing the spy brought to justice.

What if the spy wasn't Tupperman, though?

Who else could it be?

They landed in Amarillo after sweeping the area and changed to a waiting truck. Pierce was feeling the limitations of his mortal body, as they'd been a long time without rest or a decent meal. Still he drove on, at Jackson's dictate. They followed Tupperman's trail, losing it in the shifting sands of the plain. Jackson peered through the windshield, then pointed ahead.

"There."

Vultures were circling in the clear blue sky, not too far ahead.

Pierce drove to the spot, then stopped. He got out of the small all-terrain vehicle with caution. Unlike Jackson, who was already surveying the area, Pierce was wary. That they had so little information reminded him of all the ambushes on the Watchful Host.

There was a shack just ahead. Given that the birds were vultures, Pierce didn't expect to find anything good there.

"Relax. They're still in the air," Jackson said. He checked his laze, his only nervous habit. For once, the other fallen angel looked at less than his best.

But then, seeing Rumford dead inside that duffle bag had been enough to disconcert anyone.

Jackson nodded and Pierce went around to the left. Jackson crept up on the shack from the right. They stepped closer steadily and silently, then burst on the shack at once.

There was no one there.

There were marks in the dirt, though, and the dust inside the broken shack had been disturbed. Pierce moved closer to investigate. He stepped carefully, scanning the ground and trying not to disrupt anything.

"At least three sets of footprints," Jackson said. "Two sets are all muddled."

"One set is here in the cabin."

"Looks like someone's been dragged," Jackson concluded. "But the tire tracks go over those marks. The truck left last." Jackson glanced along the line of the tire tracks. "The vehicle was back there. Someone was dragged to it, then the vehicle was driven to the cabin and away to the south." He spun to look in that direction, then up at the circling birds with a frown.

"There's blood!" Pierce said, bending to examine the drops. There wasn't much blood, just a smattering in the sand.

"But where's the body?" Jackson demanded. He came to look at the droplets and frowned. "That's not enough to attract a dozen vultures. Not enough to kill anybody either."

"Someone was wounded, then dragged to the vehicle, maybe."

The two surveyed the tracks, as if willing the ground to speak.

There was a moan then, a long low moan.

"Where the vehicle must have been," Pierce whispered but Jackson had already moved.

"Help me," moaned a man who was out of sight behind a small hill. Pierce ran after Jackson. He saw the man on the ground, his lower body covered in blood. The man lifted his bloodied right hand in what looked like an appeal.

And Jackson shot him through the chest.

The laze blast threw the man backward. A puff of sand rose from the impact, but the man didn't move anymore.

Pierce pushed past Jackson, whose laze was trained for another shot. Pierce checked the body and shook his head. The diameter of the laze wound was impressive. Jackson had shot with full power and held the burn.

"He's dead," he said, looking back at his commanding officer.

"You killed him."

Jackson appeared to be defensive. "He made a move on us!"

"He was unarmed." Pierce gestured to the man's fried right hand. "Even if he had a weapon, he couldn't have used it."

"He was aiming at you," Jackson said, his voice hard.

"With what?"

"He might be left-handed."

"He doesn't even have a laze!"

"We didn't know that." Jackson exhaled, then checked his laze again. When he met Pierce's gaze, his own eyes were cold. "I defended you from attack. That's what we do."

"There was no threat." Pierce stood up and threw out his hands. "He might have known something!"

Jackson shook his head. "He was trying to kill you. I saved you." He glanced upward at the vultures, which were circling lower. "We should follow those tracks." With that, he walked back to their vehicle.

Pierce looked down at the executed man. He took a moment to check the man's pockets, not really expecting to find any identification or clues. He didn't. Why hadn't Jackson even checked? Pierce's own heart was thumping; the way it did when things didn't add up.

It was as if Jackson knew the man's identity already.

As if he'd expected him to be here.

Jackson said he had saved Pierce, but what he had really done was silence a witness.

Pierce warily followed his commander, well aware that he was alone with someone whose motives were not what they appeared to be. He was outraged by what Jackson had just done, but challenging him here, alone in the desert, would only leave Pierce dead in the sand, as well.

He pretended to accept Jackson's explanation and continued on with his commander, certain that he knew the real identity of the spy in the ranks.

The question was what Pierce could do about it.

"In both worlds, there is sound and there is silence," Kara told the unconscious Tupperman. "And harmony is only achieved when each has its due." She leaned over him, checking his pulse and his breathing. Both had become more regular in the few hours since he'd been bitten and she dared to believe that he was out of danger.

He might have been just sleeping in her bed.

It was an appealing idea.

Sousche had gone to her own home for more food. Old Sam and Bonita were still getting rid of the truck. It was early afternoon, and still hours from the time the others would gather at Kara's house. She knew that most of them would have already heard the news from Sousche.

"My mother said that," she added as she pulled a blanket over him. "But then, you probably already guessed as much."

"Or maybe I guessed that she was trying to convince you to leave room for the silence," Tupperman said without opening his eyes.

Kara's hand rose to her lips, delighted to hear his voice. He opened his eyes then and smiled at her, although he still looked weary.

"Better?"

"Not dead," he acknowledged. "I feel a bit better than that." He stretched and checked his hand, which she had bandaged, then glanced beneath the blanket. "You were determined to get rid of my pseudoskin, weren't you?" His teasing tone made it easy to respond in kind, to pretend that nothing had changed between them.

"I couldn't lift you into the truck while you were wearing it. Don't worry. I was careful with it." She gestured to the side of the room. "Everything is right there."

She'd guessed he would look first for his laze and he did.

"I recharged it," she said, retrieving it for him so he wouldn't get out of bed. Tupperman checked it, the way anyone familiar with his weapon would routinely verify its condition, then placed it on the table beside the pillow.

"What happened to him?"

"I left him, badly wounded, and took his truck. There were vultures overhead so I'm sure he's dead now."

His glance was piercing. "Are you glad?"

Kara heaved a sigh. "Yes. Did you expect me to lie?"

Tupperman smiled. "No." His gaze locked with hers and he

sobered. "Thank you for helping me. I would have died without you."

Kara's throat was tight as she watched him closely. "I had to."

"Even knowing what I am?"

"Especially so," she admitted. "I've never met a man like you."

"Nor I a woman like you."

Kara dropped her gaze to the blanket. "I meant what I said."

He simply nodded. "Is this your home?"

"How did you guess?"

"It looks like you." Before Kara could ask how, Tupperman swung out of the bed.

"I don't think you should get up yet."

"I don't think there's a lot of choice. The police will know exactly where to find us and it would be better if I wasn't here."

Kara's heart sank that he spoke only about himself, not about the two of them together. Tupperman seemed oblivious to her reaction. He prowled the perimeter of her small house, seeming to survey every detail. He looked out the windows and peered into the distance, his impatience to depart clear. He filled the rooms with his power and energy, as if her home were too small to contain him.

Kara followed him, trying to reassure him. "They won't follow us on to the reservation. There's a jurisdictional issue. They'll have to go to Albuquerque to get a waiver..."

Tupperman silenced her with a glance. "They *will* follow us onto the reservation. They will have identified you and found your home address. Whether you're a hostage or willing participant, they'll guess that we came here. It's the most obvious choice."

Kara smiled. "Except I don't have a home address."

"What do you mean?"

"There was a time when I would have said we were like Wraiths, in that we weren't in the databanks of the Republic. If those databanks still exist, we still aren't in them."

"Don't count on it," Tupperman replied, looking out the window again.

"We have no surnames. We never had palms and we never had identification beads. We were assigned numbers, but after the last custodian died, there hasn't been a replacement from the Republic."

He looked at her with curiosity. "Because they didn't dispatch one, or because one never arrived to take up his or her task?"

Kara smiled, unprepared to condemn the more radical of her people. "My number leads only to the reservation. We all know each other and the location of our homes. We have no need for streets and addresses. They say we look the same, so let them figure out which one I am. No one will help them here."

"They'll still follow us," Tupperman insisted. "I'm accused of murdering a soldier of the Watchful Host. I've evaded capture, stolen a police vehicle and destroyed it. Another man lies dead in our path, and there will be, if not actual concern for your health, then some rhetoric to that effect. You can't know what others will do when they're pressured. I have to go." He picked up his pseudoskin.

"Tell me about being a fallen angel first," she said on impulse.

He froze and looked at her in silence.

"What will I tell our child if I don't know the truth?" She saw his indecision and stepped toward him. "Old Sam and Bonita are leading a false trail and disposing of the truck. The others will be here in a few hours, and we'll go to the Eye of Glass together. This might be my last chance to know more of you, Tupperman. If you care at all, tell me."

The tension slid out of Tupperman's shoulders, then he nodded once. "Some angels volunteer to aid humanity. We choose to take mortal flesh, so that we can walk among you and try to change the future."

Kara loved that his words verified her understanding of his character. "But why are there no marks on your back? Don't the angels have scars?"

"Yes. They have diagonal scars on their backs from the removal of their wings."

"Removal?"

Tupperman met her gaze. "The surgeon of the angels slices the wings free with his fingertip, the fire in his touch cauterizing the wound at the same time." He shuddered involuntarily at the memory. "It is the first experience of pain, for each of us."

"But you have no scars."

"Not any more. I had them removed surgically, after I chose to remain. I wanted to be seen as human."

"Can you still have your wings restored?"

His expression was bleak. "I don't know."

"When did you volunteer?"

"More than a decade ago. I came with others, who have since regained their wings and rejoined the angelic host. Upon descent to this realm, we are each assigned a task." He held her gaze. "I had the chance to have my wings restored when the angels came four years ago. But I asked to stay."

"Why?"

Tupperman heaved a sigh and paced the room. He wasn't avoiding her questions anymore, and Kara was content to give him time to find the words. "I knew a man who changed my mind. Joachim was valiant, a fighter, a man who struggled to ensure the welfare of those weaker than himself. And when the angels descended that last time, I was with him."

"The night the identification beads were destroyed. The night the Oracle summoned the angels to Chicago."

The night Dionta disappeared and died. Her unsaid words seemed to hang in the air between them.

"And elsewhere. They descended throughout the Republic and healed shades. They came even to us, because I summoned them. I knew Joachim would be glad to see the shades who accompanied him healed. He had helped them and hidden them, given them work and food. He even saved me, so I owed him. That night, I thought to repay his kindness."

He fell silent then, thinking.

Or leaving space for silence amid his words. Kara knew with sudden vigor just how much her mother would have liked Tupperman. "How?"

He shook his head. "Joachim accused the angels of leaving the task half done. He said that if the angels left, even after the shades were healed, the Republic would not continue to repair itself. He said that because he knew men, he feared for the future."

"So you stayed?"

"More than that." Tupperman paused again. "Each time an angel sheds his wings and volunteers to take flesh in this realm, a star falls in his honor." Kara felt a shiver run down her spine. "I asked the entire company that had come to us to take flesh. I asked them all to volunteer and to aid mankind. And they did."

Kara was astounded. "All those stars?"

Tupperman nodded. "All those angels. They became the

Watchful Host, a force for good in the Republic."

"And you helped them."

"My cover for years was that of a police officer. My assigned task was to keep contact with a number of fallen angels and to greet those new arrivals who used a particular location as a portal. My uniform was often useful in dealing with humans and the access to information was invaluable. I'm still a police officer in New Gotham, but my cover and my true task are now the same—I work under cover and provide covert intelligence for the Watchful Host. I use my old network of contacts, at least those who chose to remain."

The angels who had descended earlier. Kara understood. "You were protecting them by leaving New Gotham behind."

"It was the only thing I could do." He pushed to his feet, his burden of responsibility apparently heavy on his shoulders. "I was the only link between the two groups. If I disappeared, there would be no way for one to find the other."

"What happens when fallen angels die? Do you have souls?"

"Yes. All of God's creatures have souls. It is the animating force within us. It is the force of the universe, the divine spark of creation that illuminates everything."

"Like pollen," Kara said, understanding. Tupperman frowned. "Everything has pollen in our view of the world, because pollen is a mark of vitality."

"And the presence of the Bright Ones." At her nod, he continued. "Angels are almost pure electricity, power, light, thought. Maybe we're even pollen." He gave her a hard look, his comment making Kara consider a new idea. "We're filled with the animating force of creation, the word and the light."

"But angels don't die?"

Tupperman shook his head. "Unless we're murdered on earth." He was grim, then, haunted by the challenge ahead. Kara went to sit beside him and took his hand in her own.

"There's more," she prompted and he nodded even as he frowned.

"There's a stone," he said quietly.

"In your clothes," Kara said, remembering. She went to his clothing and picked up the green stone that had been in his pocket. "I wondered why you had a piece of the Eye of Glass." She returned to offer it to him.

Tupperman picked it from her hand, turning it so it caught the light. "I wondered as well. After that night, after the angels left, I found it in my pocket. It hadn't been there before."

"The angels gave it to you."

"It took me a while to find out what it was, and that Trinitite only comes from here. I dreamed that I would know when it was time. I understood that I'd been given a new mission in this sphere."

"That's why you came west."

He gave her a piercing look. "I was being framed, Kara. I thought it would only be a matter of time before I was arrested and interrogated, compelled to reveal my network and expose them to danger. I chose to pursue this quest instead." He fell silent then, frowning at the stone as he worried it between his fingers.

"What aren't you telling me?"

"Lucifer challenged me to battle him for the souls of the murdered angels." He met her gaze. "If I lose, he'll claim us all forever. If I win, I'll liberate them from his grasp."

"And regain your own wings."

"Maybe." Tupperman gave her a sad smile and squeezed her fingers. "You know I don't want to leave you now, but it's the only gift I can give you."

"Not the only one," Kara said impulsively, knowing her instinct was right. "Linger just a bit longer. Let's try again to create that child. Give it another chance, just to make sure."

She could see his indecision in his eyes. He was tempted. He wanted her and he wanted to give her that child, but he was afraid of the price of waiting.

"They won't come here," she insisted. "And even if they do, I'm prepared to take the risk."

"I'm not..."

"I want to have your child, Tupperman. Once might not have been enough."

"Once could never be enough with you," he murmured with a smile.

Kara smiled, then reached up to kiss him. She didn't hold back at all, but kissed him with all the love and passion she felt. She heard him gasp. She felt his lips part beneath her assault and felt triumphant when his tongue tangled with hers. His arms slid around her, his fingers speared into her hair, and she knew that she had won this particular battle.

She wished all triumphs could come so easily, then Tupperman deepened his kiss and she was lost in the power of his touch.

IX

It was the most curious sensation.

Tupperman didn't know if he was alone or in a crowd.

He walked with Kara, her hand held fast in his own. Her hair blew in the strong cross wind, periodically brushing his skin or sweeping across his vision, like dark feathers. The night was velvety dark, the moon a shining white orb overhead. Far ahead, the Eye of Glass reflected the moon, like a black mirror in the middle of the desert.

On every side, there was silence and solitude.

Yet Tupperman didn't feel isolated or even alone. He realized that it wasn't exactly silent. Sound was more subtle than in the city, but the desert wasn't as desolate as he'd first imagined. He could hear the wind buffeting his ears and the rustle of that wind passing over the grasses. He could feel the solidity of the earth beneath his feet, even as the loose soil passed over his boots. The earth was vital here, present and powerful. The moon cast such brilliant light that it might have been midday and in the shadows, he saw myriad signs of life.

He heard birds and other creatures, rustlings and chirpings and movement he couldn't identify. And he felt the warmth of Kara's people at his back. There were maybe four dozen of them, walking as quietly as shadows behind him. He felt their breath as much as heard it. He felt the strength of their presence. They might have been part of the land and, in a way, he supposed they were. They understood its nuances, its silences and its abilities. There was a timelessness about them that struck him with awe.

A serenity filled him in this place, a quiet sense of purpose and peace that was only strengthened by his knowledge that he walked toward his final challenge. He had made the best choices he could have made. He was confident in his decisions and comfortable in his skin in a way that had never been possible before.

It was because he was with Kara.

When he saw the dark green circle of glass, its perimeter as irregular as a splash, he caught his breath.

Then Kara gasped.

"They're there!" she whispered, pointing at the Eye of Glass. She pulled free of his hand and ran toward the dark circle, and Tupperman remembered her tale of her mother and daughter.

He caught her just before she fell on her knees beside the glass. Her eyes were wide and her expression wild. She reached past him, straining one hand toward the glass. "They're there! I have to help them!"

The glass was dark, devoid of light. Tupperman couldn't understand what she meant. He was barely aware that her people surrounded her, their eyes gleaming as they watched and listened. "What do you see? Who do you see?"

"The Bright Ones. They're in the glass." Kara stole another look over Tupperman's shoulder and her expression became pained. "They can't get out. We have to help them through the portal."

Tupperman's heart clenched as he recalled his own dream.

Or had it been a portent?

A sign that he would join the others.

"Just like her mother," Sousche whispered.

Tupperman tightened his grip on Kara and turned her back to the glass. "What did her mother see?" he demanded of the older woman.

"Something in the glass. *Someone* in the glass." Sousche moved closer and stroked Kara's arm. "She could never turn away once she looked into the Eye of Glass, not until they disappeared."

"I have to help them," Kara insisted, struggling to free herself from Tupperman's grip.

And that was when he understood.

"Who else can see them?" he demanded of her people. They all shook their heads and he knew.

He caught her shoulders in his hands and looked into her eyes. "Kara, listen to me. Your mother's gift may have skipped you before, but you have it now."

"No, I don't. Dionta was the one who had the gift..."

He interrupted her sharply. "But you're the only one who can see the Bright Ones in the Eye of Glass tonight."

She stared at him in amazement, then glanced to her friends and family. Tupperman didn't see them make a gesture, but she turned back to him, convinced. He took her by the hand and led her away from the Eye of Glass, sparing a glance at the moon overhead. He could see the earth's shadow drawing close to the moon but it hadn't yet obstructed his view yet.

"You are the seer," he told Kara.

"But that means I have to open the portal," Kara whispered when they were a hundred feet away from the glass. Her people surrounded them again, and Tupperman was no longer surprised at how fluidly and silently they moved. They watched, not speaking, but their presence was both comforting and fortifying. "It's the task of the seer but I don't know how to do it."

Tupperman saw her fear of failure and knew it was unfounded. "You have the gift. The gift will guide you."

Kara shook her head.

"You said you were haunted by Derek when he was following us."

She bit her lip. "It wasn't his ghost because he wasn't dead," she agreed. "But many people sense the presence of someone they've known well in the past."

Tupperman didn't give up. "You said you felt someone walk over your grave right before Derek attacked us and tried to put us in our graves."

Kara's gaze flicked to his.

"You knew Old Sam and Bonita were arriving before they did."

"I might have heard them."

"You saw the dark one before I spoke of him."

Kara eyed Tupperman, her doubt diminishing.

"She saw a shower of gold," Tupperman said to Sousche. "Does that mean something?"

The other woman smiled and averted her gaze, as if shy. "Pollen is gold and a shower of pollen means life," she said softly.

Tupperman understood that Kara had conceived his child.

"The prophecy," he whispered and Sousche nodded. She looked through her lashes at him, a surprisingly coy expression for a woman of her age, and Tupperman found himself smiling. "We did try," he acknowledged and heard Old Sam's chortle of suppressed laughter.

"Maybe that's what gave you the power, Kara," Sousche suggested. "Maybe your children carry the gift, and you experience it only when you are with child."

"That makes no sense," Kara argued. "It hasn't been that long."

"But it's begun. Your body knows it has begun and the sight knows it, too."

"You had it before," Bonita said and Kara glanced at her. "You knew you had to leave Derek when you were carrying Dionta." Tupperman looked at the younger woman with surprise. Bonita nodded. "She said she dreamed of coming home from the hospital and Derek killing her over the child's eyes. She was afraid of him going to jail and it being her fault."

"I forgot," Kara whispered. "I thought it was just a bad feeling."

"It was a vision," Old Sam said with resolve. "They say it comes differently to every seer, but now that it has come, you must use it."

"You must open the portal," Tupperman said.

Kara frowned.

"You remember more than you know," Sousche whispered. "Think of your mother. Remember what she did. Let her guide you."

"You can do it," Tupperman said. "No one is given a task he or she can't complete."

Kara stilled in Tupperman's grasp. "Is that what you believe?"

He nodded, realizing it was true. She had the power to open the portal, or else she would not have been entrusted with the task.

It followed that he had the power to defeat Lucifer and save those souls—otherwise, he wouldn't have been granted that task.

Kara studied him, as if reading his thoughts, then took a deep breath. She smiled at him with her characteristic confidence. "I love you, Tupperman. I hope we'll be together when this is done."

"So do I. But either way, I don't regret anything."

"Me neither." She kissed him then, kissed him with a heat that warmed him to his toes. Tupperman didn't want to part from her, but he knew they had no choice. If nothing else, her kiss gave him strength for the challenge ahead.

And surmounting the obstacles together might give them the chance for a future that he craved.

They turned as one, his grip resolute on her hand, and marched to the Eye of Glass.

Overhead, the first edge of the earth's shadow touched the luminous circle of the moon.

There were dozens of them, snared beneath the surface of the Eye of Glass, churning out of the darkness far below. Kara stared in fascinated horror, uncertain what they were. They were beings; they looked like people; they had wings and they were luminous. Was it possible that the Bright Ones were the angels Tupperman had known?

It was hard to imagine Tupperman as one of these beings. There was something ethereal and insubstantial about them, as if their shapes changed with every passing moment and their figures were poorly defined.

Their anguish was palatable, though.

She managed to spare a glance to the others and knew they couldn't see the figures. They watched her or the eclipse overhead. Kara realized that if this swirling crowd had been clear to them, they wouldn't have been able to avert their gazes.

She was both intrigued and terrified by them. If she looked fully, would she ever be able to look away again? Could she not look and maintain her sanity? Her every thought and every urge drove her closer, insisted that she look, that she feel, that she experience their pain.

Before she realized what was happening, she was on her hands and knees on the Eye of Glass. She barely registered the chill of it as she stared down into its depths. Figures swam up to her, then collided with the underside of the glass. She saw their pain, then they sank down, sometimes limply, only to be swallowed by the darkness. It was frantic, though, this allure of the surface, because they came again and again and again.

How many were there? Kara didn't know.

She guessed that Tupperman's count of lost angels might be just about right.

She lost track of time, mesmerized by their endless dance.

She shivered as a reddish orange light claimed the land. The light reflected in the dark mirror of the Eye told her that the eclipse was total.

She slid her hands across the surface and whispered four words in her own language, four words her mother had used whenever she acted as a healer. Their closest translation was "long life, everything good, old age, no evil." The glass seemed to vibrate when she said the last word.

The others echoed the words behind her. She heard Sousche offer the four words to the four directions, addressing the four winds and the four mountains, and felt a quiet confidence grow within herself.

Kara began to chant, a chant that came out of the mists of her memory. It was guttural and deep, a song of chthonic darkness, one that sprang from a well inside her she could not name. It was both familiar and strange, ancient and new, but it was utterly right. Once she began, she couldn't stop. She heard the others take up the rhythm of it and wondered if they had heard it before, too.

Kara chanted with all her might, sliding down to lie across the Eye of Glass. Its chill was against her entire body. Its cold permeated her very bones. And still she chanted.

The trapped figures came to her, clustering as close to her as possible, fluttering helplessly. She saw their faces, the pain in their eyes, the despair in their expressions.

She sang louder. The voices of her people flowed into her and through her, resonating and amplifying. The chant filled her and empowered her, making her feel large enough to touch the sky with her fingertips. She rose up to her knees, well aware of Tupperman's steadying presence behind her and his voice joining with hers, and let the power of the song gather within her. She raised her hands together over her head, palms pressed against each other and was sure she stood on the cusp of something potent.

She felt a crackle, like electricity sparking from an outlet. The hair seemed to stand on the back of her neck and the wind went still. In that breath of a moment, one that might have been outside of time, Kara lowered her arms and pointed her fingertips at the Eye of Glass.

Its surface cracked. The fault line ran from between her knees straight across the circle of glass and disappeared on the far side. Dark smoke erupted from the fissure, billowing toward the moon, and Kara had a moment to fear what she had done.

Then the trapped beings began to break the glass from below. They burst through it, shattering it on all sides. They shook dark water from their sodden wings and tried to take flight.

"I'll just step in now," said a man with a deep voice. "Thanks so much for your help."

Kara spun to see the dark silhouette of a demon, a dark angel with large leathery wings and a long tail. He blew her a kiss.

Then a police vehicle, sirens blaring and lights flashing, rushed in from the north.

Lucifer was far more substantial than Tupperman recalled. The sculpted perfection of his obsidian form could be easily seen, as well as the gleam of his teeth when he smiled. His malice was tangible, too. Worse, Kara and her people could clearly see and hear him. He had gained power in this transaction.

The loosed angels screamed in anguish and Tupperman saw that they were being drawn back down through the crack. He couldn't recognize them, not in their angelic forms, and couldn't count them properly when they moved with such speed.

A foul wind had roiled out of the pit beneath the Eye of Glass, choking the air with dark smoke. Now it rushed back down into the abyss, the force of its passing hauling the lost angels with it. They flailed in the air, wounded and sickened and weak, as powerless as autumn leaves caught in the wind. Tupperman heard the clanking of chains and saw the furious flames in the abyss below.

The Eye of Glass *was* a portal between worlds, but the lost angels hadn't been trapped in Lucifer's realm.

They'd been in a limbo. They'd been shielded from hell as

surely as they had been barred from heaven, caught between the worlds in a vortex. Now that Kara had opened the portal between the realms, Lucifer intended to claim the lost angels for his own. Tupperman wasn't really surprised that Lucifer had lied to achieve his own dark ends, but he couldn't let the demon have this victory.

He also couldn't defeat him alone.

There was only one thing he could do. Tupperman threw back his head and sang the hymn of angelic devotion, the music that had filled his life before he'd shed his wings, the song that was an invocation to the divine. He sang with all his might, sang with such volume that his lungs might burst, sang so that the perspiration broke on his brow.

He wasn't sure there were any more angels in heaven to descend to earth, because there were no more stars.

Still he had to try.

He had to have faith.

To his surprise, the struggling angels took up the music of the hymn, their voices blending with his own in the ancient song of praise. It seemed to give them strength to battle against that evil wind and they rose out of the abyss again.

The police vehicles came to a halt behind him, their lights flashing over the scene. Tupperman knew there was nothing they could do but watch and maybe believe.

Tupperman sang. He heard the voices of Kara and her people joining his song, learning it as he repeated it again and again. Their voices became stronger, their will added to the power of the music, and the angels battled for their souls with greater power. He heard a voice join the chorus from the direction of the police vehicles and knew it was Pierce.

So, the Watchful Host had followed him. He drove such practical concerns from his mind. First he had to save the lost angels.

Tupperman was aware of Old Sam turning away, because that man's voice fell silent. Old Sam stared off to the northeast, his eyes narrowed, but Tupperman knew only that he had to sing.

The hymn rose in power and the eclipsed moon lit the land with strange orange light. The trapped angels gained altitude and Tupperman dared to believe they would escape.

Lucifer snarled and shouted a curse, one so filled with hatred and wickedness that it made the others falter in their song of praise. To Tupperman's dismay, a voice joined that of Lucifer.

It was Jackson. He snarled out the dark incantation of the demon, his lip curling and his handsome face transfigured. The wind from the abyss grew in velocity, tearing at their hair and clothing like a hurricane and sucking the lost angels down with terrible force.

It was horrible to see Jackson in Lucifer's thrall but before Tupperman could act, Pierce pulled his laze and aimed at his superior.

Jackson shot the other fallen angel without hesitation, and Pierce's voice was silenced as he fell.

Tupperman's song faltered for a crucial moment. He forced himself to sing louder, even as he feared it to be futile. His voice was nearly hoarse, but he couldn't stop.

Tupperman sang with everything he had left.

To his astonishment, more voices joined the hymn. He recognized Montgomery's voice and spun in wonder at the sound. He saw Joachim and his company of shades, against all expectation. Lilia and the child from the circus, Micheline, were with them. They marched toward him with resolve in their posture and in their voices, the dark silhouettes of their vehicles abandoned behind them. They'd come across the plain in darkness, their lights dimmed, but Old Sam had seen them coming.

Or maybe the wind had whispered to him of their arrival.

Jackson and Lucifer cried their curses in unison, even as Montgomery and Lilia helped Pierce to his feet. That fallen angel looked ashen but he sang again, his determination echoing Tupperman's own. The wind lashed at all of them, tearing at them as if it would suck them all into the abyss despite the fury of the music. Tupperman felt they stood in the middle of a hurricane, one that would flay the skin from their bones, then Micheline gave a cry of delight and lifted her hands to the sky.

"The stars are back!" Kara cried.

Tupperman looked up to see that it was true. Thousands of stars were coming into view, brightening and becoming larger, even as he watched. Their song had drawn the distant hosts, perhaps the archangels, and Tupperman sang more loudly in his joy.

As he watched, the eclipse began to diminish. The shadow of

the earth eased from its central position to one side of the moon. The corona of light that had shone around the shadow flared with brilliant white light. That light fluttered, like plumes of flame, plumes that grew ever larger and brighter.

The angels were descending. Their radiance grew blinding but Tupperman forced himself to watch, even as the light of his brethren heated his face. They were warriors clad in raiment of light, ferocious defenders of all that was good. The sight of them gladdened Tupperman's heart. Everything was bathed in brilliant white light as the lost angels surged skyward to greet their fellows.

A beam of light broke from the descending company. The ray was a thousand times brighter than a shot from a laze and it struck Jackson in the throat. He choked to silence, stumbling at the impact of the angel's light.

Montgomery seized Jackson from behind and flung him into the abyss. Lucifer cursed and leapt after his minion, but Jackson fell and fell, trapped by the foul wind of Lucifer's making.

Kara abandoned the song and began to chant, as she had earlier. Tupperman realized she was trying to close the portal. He joined his voice to hers, as did the others, and the fissures she'd created in the Eye of Glass steadily closed. They sealed together, creating a smooth dark surface once again. The Eye of Glass looked like a black mirror, reflecting the glory of the angels overhead.

But this time, there were dark figures struggling beneath the barrier, pounding on the underside of the glass in their desperation to be free. Tupperman caught a glimpse of Jackson's anguished expression, then the fallen angel was swallowed by the darkness.

The angels dropped lower in the sky, and Tupperman broke a sweat at the heat of their presence. As he watched, the Eye of Glass began to steam. It simmered beneath their heat and light, bubbling and seething even as it evaporated. It turned to steam, then a strong wind blew it away.

In moments, there was only the sand of the desert and its grasses waving in a steady wind, bathed in angelic light.

He'd triumphed over Lucifer.

He'd fulfilled his quest.

And now, he'd find out if his wings would be returned to him or not.

In the hidden datahub, everyone gathered in the main room to watch the biggest screen. Tag still couldn't believe it. He was that Ferris, the Ferris, and he'd removed every doubt by contacting the Oracle directly. She'd not only listened to all he had to say and thanked him, she'd greeted him with affection.

Recognized him.

And given him an access code.

Thanks to Delilah, they were watching live vid streaming from a hand-held camera. The scene was dark, the strange light of an eclipse shining over the numerous people gathered on what was apparently the circle of glass created when the first nuclear bomb had been detonated.

Trinity.

Tag had always wanted to go there. She'd always wanted to see it, to stand in the place where the history of the world had changed. She'd never expected to get as close even as this vid, and the way it moved—as the person with the camera walked—made her feel as if she were there.

It didn't seem real to be watching the angels descend, not any more real than the battle that had preceded this. But they did descend, their light mirrored in the circle of glass and one man fell to his knees before them.

Tag guessed that was Tupperman, by the way Ferris smiled in relief. A lump rose in her throat as a second angel approached another shorter man, then framed his face in angelic hands.

"I knew they would come," Ferris said, his voice tight with emotion. "I knew the angels would see everything come right."

"Why?" Tag whispered, curious about his conviction. "Because you called the Oracle?"

He shook his head, then cast her a shining glance, one that made her heart skip. He touched a fingertip to his throat. "Because they came before when the Oracle called them. They removed my tattoo and gave me a voice again."

"What was wrong with your voice?" she asked, although she knew the story.

"It was gone, thanks to the same surgery that gave me shade status."

"You have no scar."

Ferris smiled. "Because the angels healed me."

Something softened within Tag, a skepticism of others that she'd always found evidence to support. She'd doubted Ferris, because he didn't appear to be who he said he was, but she'd been wrong.

"Praise be," Tag said softly without meaning to do so. "They're healing me, too."

When Ferris reached for her hand, she welcomed the heat of his fingers curling around her own. They turned as one to watch the vid again, their hands clasped tightly together.

Joachim was so glad that he'd come west with Lilia and Montgomery. The sight of the angels filled his heart with joy and hope. Watching Lucifer banished into the abyss encouraged him that this time, their visit might lead to real change.

As he stood, his heart thundering, the angelic host touched down with ethereal elegance. Their radiance spread across the land and was reflected by the dark mirror that had been the Eye of Glass. He watched as they dropped to their knees and kissed the ground. Joachim saw a shimmer pass through it and over it.

"What are they doing?" Bonita whispered.

"Healing the earth," Joachim replied, his voice thick with emotion. "Just as they healed all of us."

They had come. They were offering hope. Joachim was filled with gratitude.

He fell to his knees and to his astonishment, one angel approached him. Joachim could feel the heat of the angel's presence on his skin and closed his eyes against the brilliance of its light.

He caught his breath at the sensation of heat in one shoulder. The angel had laid a hand upon him.

He wanted to weep with joy, but then a voice echoed in his thoughts with such astonishing clarity that he was shocked.

You were right, Joachim, that some men will always be tempted to reach too far, to sacrifice another's well being for their own. You saw and understood, and even without the gift of foresight, you realized the challenges ahead.

Joachim wasn't sure if this was a good thing or not. He had no ability to reply so simply kept his head bowed and listened.

You are the mortal man witness to this moment, Joachim. You have been chosen to see and to hear. You are the mortal man charged to teach your fellows the merit of temperance and justice.

You are blessed, Joachim, as surely as if you were of us. Use your gifts to make your world as you would have it be.

A sense of purpose flooded through Joachim, and he sensed the spark of a thousand ideas. The angel tipped up his face and kissed his brow, the imprint of the angel's lips burning on his forehead.

It was as if they sealed a bargain, the angelic host and Joachim, and he was determined to not betray their trust. He understood that they might not return again in his lifetime.

He understood that the burden for a new beginning lay with mankind.

The angel rose, its wings spreading high as its voice rejoined the angelic chorus. Joachim kept his head bent and trembled before the angels' majesty.

He was so glad that he had come. Micheline had been the one to ensure his presence, and he knew that his greatest gift was his connection with shades. He would work with them to build a better future for everyone.

It was time to establish a traveling circus, providing jobs and opportunity for shades, and spreading the joy of hope throughout the Republic.

Joachim smiled. He had his sense of purpose back, the mark of angelic blessing, and a future filled with new promise.

It was all he could have hoped for and much much more.

Tupperman couldn't hear the thoughts of his fellows since he'd taken flesh, so he was uncertain what they would do, or what they would demand of him. His heart was thumping and his grip on Kara's hand was tight. He felt rather than saw the angels turn their attention and make a welcoming gesture to Pierce.

The wounded angel limped toward them, blood running from the laze wound in his leg. Montgomery supported him on one side and Tupperman hastened to brace his other side. They half-carried

Pierce into the brilliant light of the angelic circle and Tupperman felt the tension ease out of his comrade as his pain was alleviated.

"I knew it couldn't be you," Pierce said to Tupperman, brilliant light already filling his eyes. "I just knew it."

"Thank you," Tupperman said, then smiled. "Isn't it the task of Penemue to remedy the stupidity of mankind?"

Pierce nodded at Montgomery. "The gift of Munkar is to see into the secret hearts of men," he said, then smiled at Tupperman. He grasped Tupperman's hand, shaking it in farewell. "And the faith of Turiel makes him the rock of God." Pierce shook Tupperman's hand, then Montgomery's. "Be well, my friends. You will not be forgotten."

That was when Tupperman realized the angels had no intention of collecting him. It seemed they had seen into the heart of this angel and gleaned the truth. He stood with Montgomery as Pierce was gathered into the angels' embrace, kissed on both cheeks, and surrounded by their light. He felt the heat of their love for all of creation and closed his eyes against the tide of its power.

If only all creatures could feel this abundance.

An angel appeared before him, something about this angel appearing feminine to him. She was slightly smaller maybe and filled with slender grace. She raised her hands as if to embrace him and dimmed her light so that he could look upon her.

"Raziel!" he whispered, so glad to see that she was among the heavenly host again. "It was true."

The divine spark must always return to the creator, Turiel, as you have been told. She gestured to the dark circle beneath her. *This was a lure, a chance to end what had begun, an opportunity to disguise the abyss.*

Tupperman nodded understanding. "They volunteered."

Raziel smiled. *And were given the gift of forgetfulness. Thanks to you, they have gained their just reward.*

Her light brightened again and he had to narrow his eyes, squinting as he watched the angelic host become brighter and more numerous. She flew upward and joined their fellows, the joy in her movements filling him with an answering joy.

Another angel landed before Tupperman, his wings folded around his body and his smile filled with kindness. The feathers of his wings shone as if they were made of starlight, tipped with the radiance of a thousand sunsets. His eyes were filled with the wisdom of the ages.

"Michael," Tupperman murmured and fell to his knees. He saw that Montgomery had done the same, in obeisance to the highest archangel of all. He was humbled that this great being had answered his hymn.

His words came as much as thoughts, felt more than uttered, echoing with clarity in Tupperman's mind.

It is the end of an era, Turiel, the end of the shadow cast by the last era. It is the end of a battle, one in which our kind played an unfortunate role. You and the fallen have repaired the damage that was done. I thank you for this.

Tupperman could not reply in kind, not when he was constrained by flesh. "The gift was mine to give."

But you gave it willingly, in full awareness that it might cost you all. Faith, Turiel, is the gift you possess in abundance.

Michael paused, his wings fluttering slightly. Tupperman felt the angel scrutinizing him, perhaps reading his thoughts. He erected no barrier against the right hand of God.

A moment later, Michael continued. *You should know Kara and her people will see their sky filled with stars again, for we never forget our promises.*

Tupperman smiled. He'd been right that the Bright Ones of Kara's people and his angels were the same.

All of the fallen will choose on this night, Turiel. Michael nodded at Montgomery. *Munkar's decision has long been made.* Montgomery bowed his head. *And we know yours, as well. We have a gift for you, Turiel, in thanks for your aid to those lost angels, a trust we have kept to ensure the welfare of an innocent. She is healed, as she could not have been in this sphere. We surrender this gift to you, for you may not see us again.*

Tupperman caught his breath, not daring to hope he had guessed their gift.

Michael's smile grew warmer, then he lifted and spread his wings. Sheltered before him was a small dark-haired girl.

"Dionta?" Tupperman guessed and she nodded shyly, her dark eyes flicking past him. Her features lit when she evidently realized where she was, but Michael touched her shoulder. She looked up at him with awe and love.

Blessed be, little one, Michael said, then bent and kissed her brow.

The bright red burn of the angel's kiss appeared immediately on her forehead and Tupperman knew it would fade to a port wine mark but would never disappear. The angel gestured and Dionta ran past Tupperman. He smiled at Kara's cry of delight.

The angel caught Tupperman's shoulders in the heat of his hands and kissed his cheeks, one after the other. Then he stood back, his wings arching high above him.

Blessed be, he said one last time, gesturing to Tupperman, Montgomery, and all the others gathered there. His wings beat with such sudden speed and power that they were a blur of brilliant light.

The angels rose in a dizzying spiral of light, surging into the night sky until their figures were lost in the bright white light of the full moon.

The eclipse was over. The land was clean.

And the night sky was once again full of stars.

Tupperman and Montgomery shared a smile, then they turned as one to return to the sides of the women whose love had convinced them to remain on earth.

It was time for all of them to begin anew.

AUTHOR'S NOTE

This is a work of fiction. There are no records of angelic—or demonic—involvement in the Manhattan Project. Although more than one person has compared the light of a nuclear blast to angelfire, attributing this scientific development in any way to angelic forces is a fictional construct on my part.

The beliefs of Kara and her people in this story are loosely based upon the ideas of the Apache Indians. I didn't attribute the ideas directly because my story offers only a glimpse of a complex and fascinating worldview—and one that is not entirely accurate. I modified not only stories, but the situation of Kara and her people. For example, the Apache do not occupy the area of the Trinity site, nor have they asserted a specific claim to it. My thinking was that much of this region had originally been their nomadic territory, and that they would be one group of people who saw value in it, even after it had been depopulated as it is in my fictional world. It made sense to me that in my world, they might claim it.

I chose to explore their culture and mythology because I liked the notion of Native American peoples holding the key to see the land completely healed.

The Sea of Glass does not exist. There was a large circle of glass generated by the Trinity detonation, but it was bulldozed and buried in 1952. The site is now managed by the National Park Service as a National Historic Landmark, and the glass—called Trinitite—is said to have been removed. There are several old black-and-white images of the glass, in online photographic archives, which were taken shortly after the detonation, if you are curious. There are also mineral samples of Trinitite in museums and other collections. Apparently a great deal of what is sold as Trinitite is not, so be careful if you shop for atomic souvenirs.

Finally, I also played with the timing of the eclipse. There will be a total eclipse on November 21, 2105, and that will be a Saturday. The difference is that the eclipse will happen at 2042 GMT, which will make it visible in the afternoon, New Mexico time. I moved it to the night in this story for the dramatic effect.

ABOUT THE AUTHOR

*Bestselling author Deborah Cooke sold her first romance novel in 1992–that medieval romance, **The Romance of the Rose**, was published by Harlequin Historicals in 1993 under the pseudonym Claire Delacroix. Since then, she has published more than fifty romance novels and numerous novellas in a wide variety of sub-genres under the names Claire Delacroix, Claire Cross and Deborah Cooke. **The Beauty** by Claire Delacroix, part of her successful Bride Quest series, was her first novel to land on the New York Times' List of Bestselling Books. In 2009, Deborah was the writer in residence at the Toronto Public Library, the first time they have hosted a residency focused on the romance genre. In 2012, she was honored with RWA's Mentor of the Year Award.*

Currently, she writes medieval romance as Claire Delacroix, as well as paranormal and contemporary romance as Deborah Cooke. She lives in Canada with her husband and far too many books.

Learn more about Deborah's books at her website:
• http://deborahcooke.com